This special numbered edition
is limited to 750 copies.
This is copy
634

SALOME

Mick Garris

SALOME

Mick Garris

CEMETERY DANCE PUBLICATIONS

Baltimore
❖ 2015 ❖

FIRST U.S. EDITION
ISBN: 978-1-58767-402-0
Cemetery Dance Publications Edition 2015

Salome
Copyright © 2015 Mick Garris
Dust jacket illustration by Alex Ruiz
Dust jacket design by Gail Cross
Typesetting and book design by Robert Morrish
All rights reserved. Manufactured in the United States of America

Cemetery Dance Publications
132-B Industry Lane, Unit 7
Forest Hill, MD 21050
Email: info@cemeterydance.com
www.cemeterydance.com

ONE

I thought I hated my wife. Until she was murdered.

I thought I knew her, too. Better than anyone. I still do, if it means anything.

But now the world has seen her from the inside out; the photos and video that flooded the eye of public consumption were not for the squeamish, but everybody took a peek anyway. By now, her viscera are as familiar to the great unwashed as her ephemera were to me. She was beautiful, I'll grant her that. Few would disagree. But her physical charms were forever voided by a very sharp knife.

Ω Ω Ω

I'd first met Chase at the Emmys, where she presented the Best Comedy Teleplay a decade or so ago. Her greatest fame, of course, came at the age of 14, when she played the preternaturally pneumatic 12-year-old Ellie Frazee, one of a dozen mixed-race adoptees on the timeless comedy, *The Crazy Frazees*. She had driven a nation of men into a frenzy of guilt with her just-this-side-of-naughty double entendres and poolside bikini scenes that kept the wretched show going for three years. The scandal that broke when she was impregnated by the show's married, 52-year-old Executive Producer ended his career, but only enhanced her appeal to the tabs, if not to potential employers. Pictures from the resulting abortion in Pacoima made the rounds of some of the seamier tabloids, and are easy enough to find if you just Google "Chase Willoughby" and "botched abortion". They still stand as a gruesome precursor to the end of her own life.

It was a lean year for quality in television, even more so than most, if you can believe it. I wasn't nominated, of course. Comedy isn't what I do, and they don't hand out awards to the kind of television that I write. I had just broken up with a nominated writer on *Cherry Pie*, who was in the hospital recovering from a suicide attempt, and she asked me to be there to accept the award, just in case. Her shrink was out of town, and she had no one else to turn to. I'd love to think that she tried to kill herself *because* of our breakup, but our relationship was neither so Shakespearean nor so romantic. This woman was a speed-talker who was always on, always funny, always brilliant, and always swallowing whatever she could find in the medicine cabinet. Hers or anyone else's. A guilt-ridden, nonobservant Jew, her life was all about output; nothing entered her realm of self. But the sex was phenomenal. She was as physically creative as she was mentally dexterous: a fatal combination. She finally succeeded in taking her life last Christmas, in front of a video camera, running it live on her blog. People thought it was a joke. Again, easy enough to find on YouTube, if you haven't seen it enough already.

Sorry, when I'm not working in a three-act structure, I tend to run off-topic now and then. But life's more about the tributaries than the central locations, isn't it? Mine is, at least. Especially for the last year or two.

We were talking about Chase, and how I met her, and how I grew to hate her, and how she died:

So my ex won the Emmy that night, her second, and I was tuxed up in the best monkey suit I could afford to rent at the time, and went up to accept the award for Susan. Though it had been a while since Chase had been on a series, now that she was all grown up and more gorgeous than ever, ABC was gambling on stunt casting her as a conscientious doctor having to make the decision whether or not to perform an abortion on a raped lesbian activist in a coma. It was a 6-episode arc on *Frankel's People*, and her appearance on the Emmys was to promote the show's premiere the following month.

When Chase handed me the Emmy itself, which is a lot heavier than you might expect, there was a spark of static electricity that jolted us both, and we dropped the award to the floor, where it shattered and made a horrible dent in the stage floor. The inebriated members of the Television Academy gasped as one, and everything passed in slow motion for the next few minutes. As they whisked another statuette out from backstage, handing it to Chase to hand it to me, I held it tight this time. She leaned in to give me a congratulatory kiss on the cheek—for an award that I had not won—and I could smell the lightest waft of curry on her breath. She took my hand and looked directly into my eyes with an expression that gleamed, eyes that twinkled and sparkled and changed colors under the stage lights. She held onto my hand just a little bit longer than she needed to, and I, like everyone else who was watching and had harbored the guilt of a private lust over her passing childhood, was smitten. There was nothing childish about her this night. She was sheathed in a simple black creation, slit so high up one side that underwear were not allowed. The back dipped so low that just the dimple at the top of the crack of her perfect peach of an ass was revealed. The slashed sides of the dress allowed a teasing peek at the delectable plumpness of her breasts, leading you to believe that if you stood *just so*, or if she just leaned *just this way*, you might get to see the nipples that topped them… the nipples that teased you as they proudly announced themselves from under the simple sheath of black silk.

I had been marked on the cheek by the lipstick print of her lush and sensuous mouth, and when she held my hand and led me off the stage, my heart was pounding a hip-hop anthem.

When they lead you off the stage, you are shepherded into an area where all the photographers and TV people converge to document your momentous genius. Well, it was obvious it was not *my* genius being celebrated that night, and that nobody wanted to photograph or interview me. I was standing there with somebody else's award, after all, and hell, none of these people had ever seen the show I wrote and created, or if they had, they certainly wouldn't admit to it. So I wandered the gauntlet of flashbulbs and tabloid correspondents with an admitted bitterness that I couldn't hide. Not that ET, TMZ, or GMA would ever notice, or give a shit.

Chase, however, my beautiful Chase was chum in the water, devoured by the media sharks, each one taking a bigger bite. She had not been on the air for nearly ten years, but nobody who looked like this could avoid the spotlight for long, especially with her ignominious and salacious past. *Frankel's People* was just assumed to be a massive hit.

But for some reason, after making her way through the march of shame, she saw me tippling the complimentary champagne and nibbling the cunning miniature shrimp all by my lonesome, swept up next to me and slipped her arm through mine.

"I hate this shit," she whispered in my ear, close enough that her lips touched me. The heat of her breath left me instantly aroused. "But I love *Slaughter*." That's the name of my claim to fame: a grim hourly manifesto of madness and grotesquerie that runs on a premium channel that *isn't* HBO or Showtime in the late night hours, up against the pun-titled porn for over-weight virgins, way up in the high channel numbers.

Her hair was disheveled, and there was a sheen of perspiration across her face, beading on her upper lip. I wanted to taste it.

"Thank you," was all I could think to say.

"I'm not complimenting you. I like it. I like dark shit. *Smart* dark shit."

"You'll swell my head," I told her.

"Which one?" she asked. And I was hooked. We got to know each other biblically that very night, in the marble stall of a backstage men's room at the Kodak Theater on Hollywood Boulevard, coupling desperately until we both combusted, collapsing breathless and giggling on top of the lid of the toilet, our rapture echoing throughout the room. Inelegant, yes, but accessible to the needy as well as the handicapped.

Yes, ours was a relationship founded in Eros and finalized in Thanatos. But the physical part was passionate, a ripe plum constantly devoured by the both of us, equipped perfectly to mate… except when it came to that part after the orgasm; or, in the early days, orgasms. It started with the occasional sniping that seems inevitable to some as a marriage matures. The little things that began as annoyances—sleep schedules, to procreate or not to procreate, atheism vs. a belief in God, Bravo vs. IFC, Glenn Beck vs. Keith Olbermann—soon grew into battles *royale*. Her sleep was skittish at best, light and uneasy, and she rose with the sun. On the other hand, I couldn't sleep until deep into the night, and did not rise until the clock struck double digits, as the imaginary Lord intended.

Within two years of our wedding, we lived in separate bedrooms, on separate floors, our televisions broadcasting opposite ends of the cultural spectrum. The sweetness of that naughty little teenage wet dream was corroding, and I had no doubt that it was mostly my fault. Our lives were cleaving apart, our interactions receding. Her new series turned out to be shockingly unsuccessful and the reviews were unkind at best. Chase Willoughby was inarguably breathtaking, but the charm of the fourteen-year-old Lolita did not make up for the lack of depth and acting chops when she danced well into her twenties.

After the miscarriage, any semblance of a marriage jumped off a cliff, and we never tried again to create a little human from our combined DNA. We both realized later that that was probably a good thing, for us as well as for the child, and even the planet, but at the time it was devastating.

My own writing grew darker, and *Slaughter* soon dropped from the radar of the disaffected as I endeavored to go into the independent feature world with stories even more sanguinary and hopeless than the midnight hauntings of the local Landmark Cinema. Well, there is no longer an independent film world, at least not in the professional sense. Movies today have to cost over a hundred million dollars or under a hundred thousand. And that leaves me out. No free-of-charge YouTube postings for me, thank you very much.

So we failed together and alone, and the blood of happiness drained from our marriage. Hate sex left weekly bruises, and, though I didn't think there was any extramarital fooling around—I know there wasn't on my part—we were only a couple publicly. Failure took hold like a mold, blanketing our marriage in a festering penicillin that did not heal. Her value was only to the tabloids; mine… well, I had none.

Sometimes I would look up and see her caught in the sunlight, her mind a million miles away, her face deep in repose, and see a radiance that had been the Chase that I married, the woman I'd fallen in love with, the sun backlighting her unkempt hair just so, and my heart would skip a beat. And then, as if feeling my eyes upon her, she would turn to me and her eyes would darken with such venom and resentment that I had to leave the room.

I couldn't write.

She couldn't act.

We lived together apart in a shrinking south-of-the-boulevard Woodland Hills bungalow, and all we could do was hate.

Ω Ω Ω

I'd come home from a screening at the TV Academy of a friend's pilot; it was silly and just like all the other pilots you've ever seen before, but the food was good, and it was a respite from being at home in our little emotional freezer. I chatted with my producer friend, if a producer could ever truly be a friend, putting off the trip home as long as possible. The crowd thinned as asses had been kissed and everyone saluted everybody else's genius, and it was time to leave. Resigned, I trudged to the parking structure and fell into the long, slow departure lane and the lonely drive to Woodland Hills.

The house was dark when I drove up. Chase had no doubt gone to bed by now, but that didn't explain the total darkness that enveloped our home. Night had fallen like a purple curtain. The porch light, the living room, everything was wrapped in gloom. She must have been pissed at me. Again. That's all right; I was pissed at her, too. For something. Give me a minute and I'll think of a reason.

I unlocked the door and entered the still and forlorn little house. A shiver passed through me as I saw what it once was: a little showbiz love cottage, a place where two Hollywood professionals with hope and ambition and a new start in life made passionate love and laughter. And now, all that remained was darkness and shadow. And memories, good and bad. The good ones were getting harder to recall.

I started to head upstairs, but for some reason decided to check on Chase. I tiptoed to her room on the ground floor. Her door was ajar, so I crept forward and peeked inside. Her still-unmade bed was empty.

"Bitch," I said to myself as I turned and made my way upstairs to shower off the cloak of Hollywood self-congratulatory goo.

I was pissed off when I went to bed, and just kept reading the same paragraph in the latest Carl Hiaasen, which didn't make me laugh. Cradled in champagne and Floridian foul play, the house trapped in a stillness that approached tranquility, I fell into a sleep that would not last.

Ω Ω Ω

It seemed like my eyes had just closed when the phone rang. As usual, the startling sound had worked its way into the dream that wove in my slumbering brain: a woman—Chase? But with wings that were shedding their feathers—was screaming at me, shrill and horrific, as blood poured from her mouth. I opened my eyes in the darkness and stared at my iPhone as it danced next to the Ambien bottle, not quite understanding what it was trying to say to me. As the shroud of sleep slipped off of me, I realized what it is that a telephone does, but did not recognize the number proclaimed in big white digits. It was close to three in the a.m., and I was in no mood to talk to an Unknown Caller. But thinking that it might be Chase, who might be calling because she was in trouble, I forgot that I hated her and answered the call.

It was not Chase, however, but yes, she was in trouble: trouble I could not fix.

"Mr. Turrentine?" said the officious voice on the phone, and I knew this could not be good news.

I croaked a three o'clock response.

"This is Deputy Sheriff Hardy with the La Paz County Sheriff's Department in Arizona."

No good news ever starts with "this is Deputy Sheriff Hardy with the La Paz County Sheriff's Department in Arizona."

Chase had been found murdered in a tiny, ramshackle motel on Highway 60, not far across the California/Arizona border in a flyspeck town called Salome.

I was stunned, unable to speak.

"Did you hear me, Mr. Turrentine?"

"I'll be right there." They told me that it wasn't a good idea for me to come all the way out there, but I got the information and clicked off the phone, perspiration suddenly seeping out of me, a Gordian knot of nausea welling up from within. I vomited until only empty retching remained, but even those dry heaves took a long time to recede.

It was only when I was retrieving the Beemer from the garage that I realized that Chase's Prius was missing, had been when I came home, too, but I just didn't bother to notice. My mind was a vacuum as I wound down the narrow road until I reached Topanga Canyon, during the rare three hours of quiet that settles there every night. I sat and waited at Ventura Blvd. for the light to change; silly, as there was no cross traffic. The 24-hour people that feathered in and out of the all-night Ralphs supermarket at the corner were bleary-eyed, anonymous; they looked like insects to me. Impatient, and knowing that under the New Economy there would be no police to notice, I ran through the red light and blasted onto the freeway heading east.

$$\Omega \ \Omega \ \Omega$$

Chase was dead, messily and verily deceased. It was hard to accept, or even fathom. At three in the morning, she seemed practically a stranger to me. I could easily recall the Chase Willoughby I had wooed and married, but the wife, my partner in matrimony just lived in the same house as me. The woman with whom I'd shared so many laughs, movies, martinis, waltzes, orgasms, award shows, film festivals, toasts, tears, fights, screams, and threats was drawing flies in a dumpy little James M. Cain motel in Arizona. That Chase, the dead Chase, the one who turned away rather than lock eyes with me, the woman who'd lost so much respect for me that her disgust radiated every time she was in my presence… I didn't know her. I lived with her, assumed the worst, and forgot to remember the best. Until she was dead.

I had a good five hours or so to remember her as the Beemer shot across the 210, past Pasadena, bisecting San Bernardino before I hooked up with Interstate 10, beyond the faded concrete giant dinosaurs in Cabazon, past the hundreds of lazily spinning massive windmills that skirted the outlet mall and casinos, rocketing past Palm Springs, where we had run away and become husband and wife. Even at 4:45 in the morning, the heat radiated over the desert highway, creating a mirage that resembled real life. The sun's rosy glow began to nip at the horizon now that I was leaving civilization, and I set the cruise control to 85. California has topography of every kind: verdant mountains, beaches, hill and dale, but the desert, the flat, stinking characterless desert was just a cruddy expanse of the occasional Indian casino and Denny's. The freeway was straight and monotonous, and with only an hour or so of sleep under my belt, the 740i thrumming a lulling one-note symphony, only the picture in my mind of my slaughtered wife kept me awake. In my hurry, it seemed to take days, not hours, to make my way to the scene of the crime. Even still, I couldn't bear to turn on the radio; I needed the quiet.

The scrub, ugly and gnarled at the best of times, was even more grotesque in the summertime, when it was dry, brown, and hungry. And this was not a desert of sands and dune: no, it was dirt and rock and lizards painted across the highway, the occasional greedy service station called Love's hoping you'll run out of gas and pay their exorbitant prices.

As the sun cleared the horizon, it shone directly into my eyes for the next two hours before I could get it to hide behind the visor. Blythe was the last California town before the border, and I was glad to leave that nasty little desert harridan in my exhaust. Arizona announced itself with the sudden presence of saguaro cactus standing tall and waving welcome with their thick, spiny arms. The gas gauge was ticking on empty, the fuel light flashing, its belly rumbling. I stopped in Quartzite to fuel up, and it was crowded with early morning rock hounds setting up stalls for an outdoor event. Lines of RVs driven by hunched and wizened agate collectors curled around the gas stations, keeping me from Chase; they were cranky and slow, honking their horns as they jammed in front of me in line. My engine died just as I pulled up to the pump. Kill me before I get old, okay? Oh, shit, I felt guilty once the thought flitted across my mind.

The tank was full and I sipped on a bottle of water, horned my way through the clotted arteries of Winnebagos, and shot back onto the freeway. Not far beyond lovely Quartzite, my GPS found the turnoff to Highway 60, and I was on my way.

Ω Ω Ω

Salome is an elegant, evocative name for an Arizona town, but not a particularly appropriate one for this dog turd of a burg. Much less than a town, straddling a two-lane artery along the western border of Arizona, it was the sun-baked bastard off-spring of Oliver Stone and Jim Thompson. It didn't just radiate the brutal August heat in alcoholic ripples, it *festered*. There was an ancient cowboy bar and restaurant across a parking lot of dirt and crushed gravel, with dull grey rocks that kept you from parking against the wall. A couple of decomposing motels sat under sagging faded signs begging for your business. The most inconvenient of convenience stores sat at its one intersection, with a couple of furious, emaciated dogs tearing noisily at one another's ears. A couple of Mexican men shaded by dirty, once-white vaquero hats were laying down dollar bills on the dirt as the battle continued and blood was spilled. The place smelled like rotten eggs, even with the Beemer's vents closed. There was no residential area that I could see; not even so much as a post office.

The sign for Salome reads "where she danced." Frankly, I could not imagine such a dance taking place here, with or without the veils, though I could easily work up the image of John the Baptist's decapitated head being served up on a tray.

But most of the activity in Salome now was centered at Sheffler's Motel, a dilapidated shithole announced by a long-peeling sign and anchored by rusting pickup trucks on blocks and billboards proudly proclaiming ice cold beer and special family rates. The only family I could imagine taking a room here was Manson's.

Three Sheriff's cars and an ambulance were parked haphazardly in the wide dirt lot when I pulled in. I set the emergency brake, took a deep breath to batten down the sudden pounding of my heart, and stepped out into a blast of 120-degree heat, just as the EMTs carried my wife's sheet-bound corpse out of one of the little rooms on a stretcher. The linen wrapped around her was soaked with her crimson blood.

As I stood from my car, Salome did indeed dance around me, as I was instantly dizzy, caught in the climate change from air-conditioned BMW to Arizona blast furnace. My first breath of the scorched air was enough to dry my windpipe and lungs and make me hack.

Fighting vertigo, I rushed from the car to stand in the way of the gurney to keep it from being loaded up into the ambulance.

"Wait!" I cried. They looked up with grumpy, work-to-do faces. "That's my wife."

They stopped and stood there, casting a look at the motel room. A crowd, well maybe a dozen people, but surely a crowd by Salome standards, stood sweating in the heat of the parking lot behind the crime scene tape, sipping from bottles of water and beer, one of them popping pictures with his Instamatic; none of them had mobile phones. This was the event of the season here in the desert. Most were men, grizzled and craggy, mainly but not exclusively Latino. They had lived hard lives. The few women were either massively overweight and heavy-breasted or emaciated, puffing on brown cigarettes. There were two or three dirty, barefoot kids of about five or six, one of them holding an iguana to her chest.

One of the EMTs behind the gurney, a tall, gawky, alarmingly white-skinned kid with pink eyes and white eyelashes, told me to talk to the Patrolmen. As he spoke, two deeply tanned men emerged from Room 4, putting their mirrored sunglasses on as they stepped into the searing light of day, just like in the movies. The larger, more muscular of the two looked up at me.

"Mr. Turrentine?"

There was no question who I was. Beemers don't stop in Salome; they pass through as quick as they can.

"Sheriff Hardy."

He nodded curtly, and his beefier, shorter *compadre* was happy to leave the business to his partner.

"Thanks for waiting." As if they'd been hanging around waiting for me to show up.

"We're just wrapping up the scene, Mr. Turrentine." He looked a little upset that I'd arrived before he had gone back home to Phoenix. "There really was no need for you to come here, sir."

"She's my wife. I assumed you'd want me to identify the body."

"There's no doubt about the identity of the victim, Mr. Turrentine."

A silence as hot and dry as the gust that kicked up passed between us.

"I… I'd like to see her."

Hardy looked at his partner, who looked away.

"You sure about this?"

"If it was your wife, what would you do?"

Hardy sighed. "It's not a pretty sight."

"I don't expect it to be."

I could only see my own face reflected in his movie-cop sunglasses as he stared me down, but I could see the crinkles form around his eyes as he squinted at me. The EMTs were watching him expectantly. Knowing better than to argue, or maybe just not having the energy, Hardy took a deep breath, blew it out like a bull through his capacious nose, and nodded to the gurney handlers.

Now I wasn't so sure I wanted to see Chase this way, and stood frozen for several seconds.

"You sure?" Hardy asked again.

Girding my courage, I nodded and stepped over to the head of the gurney, the bloody sheet going brown and dry as it hit the broiling sunlight. I looked up at the rangy, pimply albino med tech, and he looked away from me, taking the edge of the sheet and slowly, respectfully, lowered it to reveal her face, as the simmering crowd of Salomean onlookers eased forward as one.

I closed my eyes, breathed, and looked down at the face of the woman I had once loved.

My heart stopped. Despite Hardy's warning, I had no idea it would be this upsetting, this horrific. Her face had been deeply slashed from forehead to windpipe, her nose hacked off and her once wide, elegant blue-green eyes punctured, leaving red-black holes in their wake. This monstrous corruption of human beauty was more than I could take, and I must have lost consciousness.

The next thing I knew, Hardy, whose touch was surprisingly gentle and respectful, was helping me to my feet. The EMTs were loading the gurney through the open vehicle doors, and I snatched a final glance of Chase's covered body—its center thick and wet with drying blood—as it was devoured by the back of the ambulance, its mouth slammed shut in finality.

"I warned you."

He had. But I thought I could take it.

It was an image I cannot shake to this day, one that defies understanding. I have hated in my life, had even hated this very being that was on its way to a morgue somewhere, but I could not possibly fathom the depth of the savagery that had been unleashed against my wife. Is a respect for life what makes us different from animals? Here was savagery more vile than any perpetrated by any of nature's beasts against another: intentionally wicked, bloodthirsty, this had nothing to do with self-preservation. This heinous brutality had been unleashed in a fury of passion. Whoever sliced up this ethereal goddess had obviously enjoyed the act. Even at the highest peak of my mountains of madness, I could not imagine a brutal fury capable of such an act. It reminded me of nothing more than poor Catherine Eddowes, Jack the Ripper's next-to-last known victim, whose mutilations had been carved in a seemingly similar frenzy.

"When did this happen?" I asked Hardy.

"We think sometime after midnight."

"Do you know who did this?"

"Not yet. But I promise you we will."

"I want to believe you."

He shrugged.

"You want some coffee?" he asked. I nodded, still woozy in the Arizona sun. I suddenly realized that the adrenaline had quickly fled my body; the heat was surging, and my desiccated larynx started to wheeze.

"I would," I told him. And he led me across the street.

"You okay?"

"No," I said. "Definitely not okay."

He grunted, then led me to the edge of the road, as a cluster of three recreational vehicles lumbered past, trailed by dervishes of red dirt. Once the behemoths had trundled past, he led me across the blacktop.

TWΩ

The spouse is always the first suspect. You feel guilt regardless of how far you are from the scene of the crime. As I had been sledgehammered by the potent cinematic reveal of my dead wife's slashed-open face, I could not help but feel complicit, that our mutual and growing hatred had somehow taken root and led to this. I knew it wasn't true in a legal sense, but I felt dirty with responsibility regardless.

Of course, the slaughter in Room 4 had taken place at a time when it was impossible that I could have been anywhere nearby. It was a five-hour drive from Los Angeles, I'd been seen by hundreds of witnesses at the TV Academy Theater, I'd been called at home and wakened around three in the morning. Still, my stomach roiled.

There is no police station in Salome; hell, there's not even a Starbucks. Christina's Restaurant and its adjoining Cactus Bar stand as the pulmonary center of town. A faded, classic Southwestern adobe desert outpost, it has withstood scorching heat and wind for nearly a century. A 10-year-old Kia sat on mismatched tires in the parking lot, next to a 1962 Rambler station wagon, completely stripped of its factory paint job, but also, somehow, clean of rust. A twenty-year-old Harley leaned against the wall. Cute, vintage weathered wooden signs offering terse knee-slappers like "laughing gas, a smile with every gallon", and "Arizona roads are like Arizona people: good, bad and worse" were nailed up around inept and peeling desert landscape paintings on the walls. The Cactus Bar was not open for business, but the door was wide as the floor was being hosed off in a torrent of vomit and cheap beer, and the peek within was a glimpse into somebody's nightmare of the past. The bar itself was ancient, wooden, spectacular, and the modern neon beer signs were at odds with the kitschy cowboy clutter and worn, upholstered Naugahyde. It was gloomy and dense with knickknacks, and decades of tobacco smoke covered the wall in a gummy grey lacquer.

Hardy led me next door into the restaurant side, which at least was sunny. Though not large (what could be in this miniscule apology for a town?), it was spacious, with a big U-shaped counter surrounding the grill. The place had just opened for business, and a couple of old-timers sat slurping at thick, chipped ceramic mugs of coffee, sucking on cancer sticks. You can still smoke in restaurants in the great state of Arizona, where time and civilization stand still. The stench of bacon and eggs was enough to choke on… and I did.

All eyes were on me as we walked into the bright yellow room. We took two of the upholstered red vinyl stools at the counter; the duct tape patches were curling and sticky, and the stools rocked precipitously, so I sat with caution. The waitress, stuck in the 1940s, had bright red lipstick that crept into the smoker's crevasses that radiated around her mouth, and hair that had been dyed a jet black, piled up in a bluff over her furrowed brow. Osteoporosis curled her back, but she proudly displayed her ample bosom in a push-up bra that acted as titty bowls, offering up her quivering, age-spotted, stretch-marked breasts in proud display. If she was working her assets for tips, it would be a while before she made the rent. Her smile was amateur artifice, broadcasting capped teeth with grey ridges, yellowed by her Tareytons. She gingerly laid a menu in front of me and greeted Officer Hardy.

"Mornin', Billy, hon. Scrambled, bacon crisp, pumpernick-el dry?"

"Just coffee for me, Jackie. Mr. Turrentine?"

The smell of eggs curdled an already off-kilter stomach. "Just coffee, thanks. Black."

"Got us a new blueberry pie Jimmy just brought down from the Costco. Looks mighty nice. Talk you into a slice?"

"Sounds good. Mr. Turrentine?"

"Just coffee."

My energy had collapsed. Having seen Chase's ravaged body had left me feeling like the corpse. My hands had been cramped and shaky since letting go of the steering wheel after five hours, but they were settling now. I could feel exhaustion creeping me over like a predatory cat. I felt heavy, sunken, de-flated.

The two cowboys at the table by the window kept throw-ing glances my way, but nobody spoke. They knew who I was and why I was here. Jackie turned on the radio to fight the oppressive, stuttery silence, but if I were scoring this scene, I wouldn't have chosen "Tie a Yellow Ribbon", even for ironic counterpoint. Jackie served up the promised diner coffee, and it was better, darker, stronger and more potent than it had any right to be.

I stared at Hardy's hands, and they seemed remarkably soft and young. His job must not require much physical activity, despite the fitness of his body.

"Do you know how it happened?" I asked him.

He took a deep breath and stared into his coffee.

"We've dusted, photographed, spatter-patterned, and blood analyzed the whole scene. All of those tests will be conducted in Phoenix, quickly and carefully, by a very competent staff."

"I don't doubt your competence; I just want to know what happened to my wife."

"So far as we know, she was in the room when her life was taken. It was a brutal killing with at least one very sharp blade."

"I saw her face. But it seems the sheets were hiding a lot more."

Hardy sipped his coffee and nodded.

"What else?" I asked him.

He really didn't want to talk about this with me. And he was right. It was horrid.

"Whether I can take it or not," I told him, "I need to know. I'll find out anyway."

"I'd opt for later if it was me."

"I don't want to hear about it on CNN."

Hardy took off the mirrored shades and turned to me. His eyes were alarmingly small and deep-set, and of a blue so icy they were almost clear. But though they were tiny, they radiated an intelligence he was loath to proffer. I knew better than to pick a fight with him. He locked eyes with me, apparently trying to peer into my soul to see what I could handle. I'd already passed out in front of him, and I'm sure he didn't want to have to keep picking me up off the floor.

I just stared at him, fear and repulsion eating away at my stomach lining, but needing to know anyway.

He blinked.

"She was eviscerated, her body opened up and the organs displayed. Her breasts were slashed open, and her face was disfigured in a frenzy. The walls and the bed were covered in her blood. The room was not booked; in fact, there were no customers staying at Sheffler's, so the manager had gone home at about ten. Apparently whoever killed your wife broke into Room 4 and, and... had their way with her behind closed doors."

It was like being hammered by Ali, one blow after another to the head and gut. I couldn't look at Hardy, and by now he couldn't look at me. It didn't stop Jackie, who hovered as close as she could as she served up the hunk of pie to hear all the gory details, staring cataract-clouded holes through me.

I could hear my heavy, thudding, rushing pulse pounding through my ears.

"You made me tell you..." I waved him quiet.

"Was she... was she raped?"

"There was no seminal evidence of such an event. We'll know more after the tests are completed."

"And nobody saw anything, what kind of car they arrived in, heard noise from the room?"

"We're doing our job, Mr. Turrentine. No witnesses have come forward yet, but it's early. We'll find him. I can promise you that."

It was an empty promise. Too little too late. And nobody should ever make promises they can't keep.

"Go home, Mr. Turrentine. There's nothing more you can do here."

He was right, I guess. But I couldn't just drive out here for five hours, see the hacked and slashed body of the woman I once loved, then drive home. Aside from the exhaustion, my wife's blood kept me here. Our pulses had once beat in synchronicity, our fevers had risen together. I could not abandon the life that she'd spilled so copiously after a mere glimpse of its empty vessel.

"I've got your mobile, right? If there's any news at all, I will give you a call right away."

Ω Ω Ω

I—and the dozen or two humanoid vultures that crowded around the crime scene tape—watched as the three marked County Sheriff's cars pulled out of the gravel lot, evaporating in the morning sun. Room 4 had been evacuated, left hollowed but newly painted in Chase's blood. As the cop cars eased up Highway 60, out of Salome toward Phoenix, I looked down to see that I cast no shadow.

Once the law had left, the townspeople had nothing to look at but me, and I became the monkey in this zoo. They kept their distance, but could not keep their eyes off of me. It was uncomfortable for me, the writer, to suddenly be the center of attention, and I withered under their inconsiderate stares. Exhaustion had caught up with me and made me its mate. The hour or so of sleep had not made a dent in the inertia that suddenly took me over. I stared at my car, which was still ticking as it rested in the middle of Sheffler's parking lot.

"Go home," Hardy had told me. Driving another five hours across the monotonous blacktop was the last thing I was capable of doing now. I looked up at the hungry sun, down the deserted highway, across the sea of faces seeking distraction from their tedium, and felt nailed into place. Before I could allow the sun to melt me, I made my way to Sheffler's office.

The manager, maybe Sheffler himself, I don't know, had rheumy eyes magnified by thick glasses wound with adhesive tape, and a bald, shining skull with some kind of lump or tumor on its crown. Tufts of tight, curly grey hair nestled in the caverns of his ears, and he wore a Hawaiian shirt bedecked with Route 66 signs all over it. His limbs were long and bone-thin, though his stomach was round, distended, voluminous. The stench of his breath hinted of late-stage cancer.

"I'd like a room, please," I told him. It was as if I'd shot him.

"It was my wife who was killed here, this is the last place I'd want to stay, I was you." He just kept shaking his head, like I'd asked him to take a bite of my shit.

"You know, we was closed. Denny had already gone home. They must've busted in or something. We can't do nothin' about somebody breaks in when we're not even here." Maybe he left out words because he didn't want to waste what time was left for him.

"I'm not blaming you," I told him again. "I just need to rest. I've been up all night."

He kept shaking his head as he got me the key. "Me, I think you're nuts, but it's your picnic, ain't it? How 'bout Room 1? Furthest place from the scene of the crime. You mind moving your car to one of the designated spaces?"

Ω Ω Ω

Room 1 was a toilet. It had last been decorated around the time we won the war… and you know how long it's been since we won a war. There were dusty framed "paintings" of horses and flowers nailed to the walls, and the anemic single bed sagged like an aging nag about to be put out of its misery. The tattered curtains wouldn't discourage the dim light of a bad idea, and the door wouldn't even close all the way. When I finally just collapsed on the bed, a cloud of dust settled over me as the bedsprings howled in protest.

It felt better to be horizontal, though my head swam in fatigue. I closed my swollen eyes, and my head throbbed with an ache I hadn't noticed until now. I knew that Room 1 was fateful in Hitchcock's *Psycho*, but for me, it was respite from the sun, a bed to crash in, a rest stop between interstate journeys. Sheffler's was thankfully devoid of taxidermy, unless you counted the sawdust and sand that had replaced my brain.

As I lay there waiting to drown in sleep, all I could see was the corruption of Chase's beauty, its lovely features and her very femininity that had been so violently violated, destroying an inarguable, God-given beauty and sending it to hell. The lushness of her very womanhood had been purloined. As I lay there in a near-dream state, feeling like the bed was spinning and about to be sucked down a drain, I started to forget why I'd hated my wife. I remembered her smile, so rare of late; her teases; her tender kiss goodbye the first time she had to leave for a location shoot in New Mexico; our first night in our brand new Woodland Hills homestead; the California king-sized bed that became our own personal DMZ in those early days. The fights, though their memories would return, often but more distant, fell away, and I wept in sorrow.

But sleep… sleep would not befriend me this day. It teased me occasionally, but just as I was about to fall into its abyss, it pulled away from me, left me with open eyes and pounding heart. It knew I wanted it badly, and was just being an asshole. Nerves vibrating and my brain overloaded, I went into the bathroom and took a shower instead. The water alternated between scalding and room temperature before it gave out entirely, leaving rusty soapsuds swirling down the tub's fetid drain. I could imagine Janet Leigh's unblinking eye glaring back at me.

I toweled off in a strange state of disassociation, removed from my surroundings but somehow moving through them. As I dressed, I saw Sheffler, if there was indeed a Sheffler here, heading across the street to Christina's. Knowing that sleep was hopeless, I waited behind the peeling door until he entered the diner, then opened it and stepped back out into the baking Salome sun.

The gawking crowd had dissipated when the Highway Patrol took their leave, so I was alone as I trod the gravel of the parking lot. An unhealthy curiosity drew me to Room 4, which was draped in yellow crime scene tape. The crime had been committed and documented, so I felt no compunction about taking a look. Trepidation, certainly, and the heartsick nausea that hung from me like a shroud, and the need to see how and where Chase had spent the last moments of her life drew me inexorably to reach for the doorknob and give it a turn.

It wasn't locked, which could have been why the killer had chosen it. The door opened with a raw creak.

I lifted the tape and stepped under it and into the room with the curious sunlight, knowing I shouldn't.

Once in the room, I froze. As the rusty, rotting smell of spilled blood simmering in a closed, stifling box of a motel room reeked around me, my eyes adjusted to the lack of light, but only let in more darkness.

There was a double bed in the middle of the room, which was slightly larger than my own. Blood, lots and lots of blood, seemingly gallons of it, surely more than one petite woman could hold, had seeped into the mattress. The browning substance had spattered two of the walls in hideous dark art. Without warning, the contents of my stomach suddenly lurched up and I vomited on the floor, despoiling whatever active crime scene might remain here.

I was done with Salome and the veiled secrets she held. I left the sticky battleground of Room 4, reeling in heat, exhaustion, and nauseous sorrow, and climbed back into my Beemer.

Ω Ω Ω

I must have fallen asleep behind the wheel in the parking lot. Dreams had pinched and taunted me with screaming faces and rivers of blood. I came conscious with a jerk to the sounds of tires on gravel on either side of me. Two television remote trucks had pulled into Sheffler's, and they disgorged competing Barbie and Ken dolls, each wielding phallic microphones my way, demanding sound bite blowjobs.

"Mr. Willoughby! Mr. Willoughby!" the generic blonde news bimbo shouted at me. "Do you have a statement about your wife's murder?" I guess I had always been Mr. Chase Willoughby, but this was the first time it had been shouted at me, as her cameraman shoved his lens right up against my windshield. The half-witted jock in a J.C. Penney's suit and tie came around the other side with *his* cameraman, fighting for my attention. Oh, to have been pursued this way by producers…

I fired up the engine and peeled out of the lot. With any luck, I knocked them all to the ground.

They did not pursue me.

Ω Ω Ω

Back on the road, Chase's murder grew more real, its mystery more baffling. Chase Willoughby could be maddening, petulant, intractable, and self-centered, but I could not think of a reason for anyone to kill her. Divorce her, yes, leave the room rather than face her ire, maybe. But to rip her up and destroy this creature seemed unfathomable to me, the one who hated her most.

But as I drove, the malevolent Arizona sun now at my back, all that animosity melted away. Maybe I never really hated my wife. Maybe she just drove me mad.

Maybe I would miss her.

THREE

I rolled over and looked at the clock. 3:32 a.m. Fuck!

I could tell that my sleep was over for the night. It had been so evasive of late, and I missed it. I knew I was growing grey circles under my eyes; just what I needed: another reason not to be cast.

He was watching television downstairs again. When the hell would he just give up and go to bed? It was the typical soundtrack: screams and screeching electronic strings, murder, violence and mayhem. Jesus, if you're going to be up at 3:30, then why don't you just *write*?

I tried not to get angry, but it was getting impossible. This house, once so cozy and embracing, had become my prison, and James my warden. Sure, I could leave whenever I wanted, but whenever I came back, he'd still be here.

Ω Ω Ω

I remember that night at the Emmys like it was somebody else's dream. A friend—well, a guy who would not take no for an answer, so kept pushing my buttons—had given me the box set of *Slaughter*, and I'd watched them all on a rainy LA weekend. It was sick and twisted, but there was an ironic intelligence behind it. It tried hard to be transgressive, and it was, but it was funny, too, in its sick and twisted way. Lots of blood, lots of viscera, but in a way that didn't piss you off. Well, it didn't piss *me* off, anyway.

And there he was that night, dressed in a tux and really quite handsome. He seemed removed from this horde of ass-kissing Hollywood automatons, a true outsider—especially having just watched the complete *Slaughter*—and the fact that he seemed like he'd rather be anywhere else was kind of a turn-on.

The *Frankel's People* costume designer had really done me up for the show, and I felt exposed, naked. I was sick of having fifth-rate, sixth-billed series bit players offering the world as they spoke to my chest. The transparent bullshit of money-grubbing, lowest-common-denominator entertainers had left me enervated. It was getting impossible to paste on that shit-eating grin and make it through another event honoring a bunch of people I've never heard of flogging shows I'd never even consider watching.

And here I was again, one of them. How do you spell self-loathing?

I knew I looked good; I'm not stupid. But that didn't mean I was offering myself up for sale. And I wasn't Ellie Frazee anymore, no matter how hard they wanted me to be. I'd grown up in body and mind, but they all wanted the former. I felt like I was a dirty joke, the girl from Nantucket. I'd had my fingers burned more than once on the Hollywood stove, but a girl has to make a living; you make your best choices from what is offered to you. My savings from *Crazy Frazees* was long gone, and the traffic accident that claimed both my parents, my rare, loving, devoted parents, left nothing but deep pockets of debt and an end to romance. I knew I wasn't going to make a living off my painting, and *Frankel's People* looked like it might actually be kinda good. So here I stood, painted and plumed and perched upon 6-inch Manolo Blahniks, presenting some kind of award to someone I didn't know, and certainly didn't care about.

The winner wasn't there to accept, and in her place was somebody, well, *interesting*. Yes, he was handsome, but not in that interchangeable pumped-up Equinox-sculpted, Red Bull-swilling, Hollywood Boulevard tabloid-courting, capped-and-saber-toothed, ego radiating, Special Guest Star, vacuous, insufferable intellectual midget that continued to throw himself at me and anyone else with breasts and a few credits kind of way. No, he looked like he was unshaven because it wasn't important to him, not because it would look good and arty. He was uncomfortable in his tux, and it looked it. And the look we exchanged on our way to hand off the statuette seemed to signal that we'd both rather be anywhere else. When we touched for the first time and there was a *literal* burst of electricity, I felt that it actually might have meant something. Or I wished that it did.

Besides, he was a *writer*, a *good-looking* writer, if that's not an oxymoron. And I had just been introduced to his oeuvre, and it impressed me. It wasn't about the same old same old; it was smart and weird and different, and rarely led to a happy ending. Did I love it? No. But it intrigued me, and that night, so did he. I was in the mood for intrigue, which is in rare supply at events like the Emmys.

Yes, I'm embarrassed by how we got to know one another biblically that night; I'd certainly never done anything like *that* before, but I didn't regret it, either.

That took a while.

I loved Jimmy, and I respected him... which is one of the reasons *why* I loved him. It thrilled me when I'd curl up in his arms in that big bed and he would read me the pages he'd just written. It was sweet and sexy and intimate in ways I'd never known before. The sex was good for a while, but that didn't matter so much to me. I'd had more than my share from the time I was fourteen. And the abortion affected my plumbing in ways I never wanted to discuss with anyone.

It hurt when *Frankel's People* was such a disaster. Not because they stopped booking me on Leno and the magazines and blogs quit photographing me, but because I was no longer busy, surrounded by funny, talented people trying to make something special in a wasteland where mediocrity is something to aspire to. I didn't *need* to be on TV, but it was fun and fulfilling to have a home. It was kind of old-fashioned and silly, I guess, but I was glad to have a husband to go home to. I wore my wedding band as golden shield.

Soon it was back to humiliating myself at audition after audition. I know I'm not a great actress, but I work hard at it. With classes and coaching, I'm hoping that I can be good enough to snag a role with some meat on it.

But as I continued to swim my way upstream, things seemed to change around the time *Slaughter* was cancelled. Here we were, now matching Hollywood clichés: the out of work actress who'd really rather be a painter, and the brooding, handsome Hollywood writer whose seldom-seen series had been cancelled, tossed aside to make room for more clutter from the cookie cutter. You'd have thought it would have brought us together. It was painful how far it threw us apart.

It's like James had just given up. Here was a ferocious talent that was sexier than any steroid-enhanced Muscle Beach bum, an intellect that was powered by a dark imagination that liked what it found when it peeked under the rocks. What I wouldn't have given to be so perceptive and verbally dexterous and complex.

My blessing had also been a curse. I've been told I'm beautiful for as long as I can remember, certainly since early childhood. And that's great, of course, to be thought of that way, whether it's true or not, and it's been a part of my life for so long that maybe it is. You get treated special, and I can't argue that it's an advantage. But it has also come to imply that vacuousness is a part of the package, that with an appealing appearance is the expectation that you're spoiled, shallow, more concerned about designer goods and cosmetics than intellectual achievement and acuity. Being admired for the shape of the breasts that just happened to grow that way, a face that was formed in a way that humans find attractive, left me feeling that my external self was all I had to offer. The preening gym rats with shaved chests and plucked eyebrows and waxed pubes with their penis-replacement Maseratis and room temperature IQs had no books on their shelves, only multiple copies of their promotion reels on DVD. When your favorite work of art is the mirror, it's time for me to call for the check.

I paint because it's something I can do on my own, and it gives me pleasure… even if I know I'm not very good at it. But I pursue it in the hopes that I'll get better.

James, however, was born with a true gift, and rather than feed it and nourish it and build it into what it could *really* be, he let Hollywood tell him that he didn't know what he was doing. When his series finally crashed and burned, he took it personally, and just couldn't motivate himself. He let the industry tell him he was shit, and he believed them.

I did everything I could to encourage him, to tell him how brilliant he is, to try to be the muse that he had called me in the early days of our relationship, but he turned away, watching movies rather than writing them, gaining weight and growing his hair, shaving a couple times a week, usually when he was being interviewed by some fat, pimply 20-year-old kid for some website or magazine you've never heard of.

I thought he was beautiful in the beginning, but his beauty faded when he abandoned what he was. I thought he was so special, so deep, so caring. But when he quit writing, I think he quit loving, too.

It seemed as if he were reduced to playing the part of the high-minded *artiste* outsider, the Man in Black, a caricature of a cynical, loft-living LA genius. It was hard to hide my disdain for what he had become, my lack of respect for him as he spent his days reading and watching movies on the 60-inch plasma. His inertia and growing slovenliness made him so much less attractive that our lovemaking grew less frequent, and much less satisfying. I submitted when I had to, and resented him for my weakness.

After I lost the baby, I never wanted to have sex again, not just with James, but with anyone. I reverted within, and happiness and I had lost our friendship.

Sleep has been difficult for me as long as I've been an adult: when it snatches at me, all it takes is a single thought to pull it away. My mind races when I'm in bed, and if I dare try to think about going to sleep, my cause is lost for the night. I will wake at the crack of dawn, no matter how tightly the curtains are closed, so I do my best to get to bed early. Unfortunately, James is a night-owl, a writer trained to do what he does after the sun goes down, a vampire of letters, when he would bother to compose. So even from the beginning, sharing a bed was less than ideal. But in the beginning our newfound love and its exhilarating and overwhelming acrobatic romance cured all ills. Sex, which had been so curdled by the abortion after Peter Garrity had knocked me up and killed my career, was fun and extemporaneous and exciting again. But only for a while.

When I lost my respect for Jimmy, I lost my desire for him as well.

And so there we were in our mutual misery, living not only in separate rooms, but separate floors, each occupying a solitary bed, our dreams stripped of eroticism and replaced by regret.

I had never been so lonely.

Ω Ω Ω

James asked me if I wanted to go to the screening at the TV Academy in North Hollywood, but I just couldn't bear the thought of painting on my Hollywood face and trading chit chat with the Botox brigade again. Yes, it might have been good for my career—and Jimmy's—to hold hands and hobnob with the network brass, the producers, and all those potential employers who would no doubt be in attendance, but I just couldn't think of a worse way to spend the first night of my period. So James slammed the door, peeled away in his repulsive giant Gila monster of a car, and I threw back four Ibuprofen and went into my studio, where I started pencil sketches of two faces tearing apart from the same body, before I realized that I was doing another primal scream. I couldn't bear to repeat myself like this, so I assembled a bunch of knickknacks from around the house and started a still life, instead.

But it was shit. It was all shit.

This house, which I had so loved, was a prison. My marriage, which had so filled me with happiness and eager hopes for a fantastic new future, had become a deadening present, a life stuck on a treadmill that needed oil. More than anything, I wished that if I couldn't have a baby, at least I had a dog.

I put on my running togs and jogging shoes and left the bungalow that harbored so much pain.

Ω Ω Ω

It was a rare summer sky framed by the hills behind the house. Giant cumulus clouds formed cotton candy animals across its expanse. I jumped into the Prius and headed across the Valley to the hillside park I used to frequent when I had the house in Sherman Oaks, way back in another life. I pulled my hair back in a ponytail and wore those giant, Fearless Fly, Angelina Jolie privacy sunglasses, and felt anonymous in my baggy T-shirt and shorts. It was an atypically cool August evening, and I just wanted to blow off some steam before they shut down the park at dusk. The Fryman trail was nearly deserted, which was fine with me. I liked it when there was no eye contact, anyway. The last thing I wanted to encounter here was an Ellie Frazee fan. There seems to be an inexhaustible supply of them in the Valley.

My thighs burned as I made my way up the steep slope that started the trail, but it was a good burn, a punishment that I felt I deserved. I was working up a sweat already, despite the unseasonably mild temperature. Big, puffy clouds were going pink as the sky purpled, daylight ebbing away. It looked more like fall than August; summer skies in LA were usually cloudless. This sure beat the elliptical machine at home in the bedroom. It was just what I needed, at least for the moment. My greater needs would have to be attended to later.

Having made the two-and-a-half mile loop, I returned to the parking lot energized, practically reborn despite my exhaustion. As I climbed into my car, I heard a voice calling my name. It happens a lot, and I've found it's best to ignore it. It's never anyone I know, anyway.

But this time it was.

Toni McLoughlin came trotting over to the car, her eyes bright, and she seemed genuinely happy to see me. The glow of her late afternoon workout looked good on her, despite her inability to tan. She gave me a big hug and asked how I was doing. I couldn't answer her. How I was doing was badly, but I wasn't about to tell her that. Words stopped in my throat before they could find a way out. I couldn't say anything, not even the mindless, meaningless chatter that passes for conversation in LA.

She could see that something was bothering me, and the smile slipped from her face. At her expression of concern, my eyes filled with tears. She took my hands in hers.

"What is it, Chase?"

I just shook my head. What it was was me. My life. Another skid mark on the bloodied streets of Hollywood. I hadn't seen Toni in a couple of months, but she was as close a friend as I supposed I had. It hit me at that moment that, though I knew a lot of people, I didn't really have any friends. I had a husband I'd grown to despise, a manager, an agent, an attorney, and a couple of neighbors I chatted with once in a while, as well as passing acquaintances, but no one I considered a true friend, no one I could turn to in an emergency, no one to whom I could open my broken heart. James used to be that friend, but it had been a long time ago.

Toni and I had worked together on *Frankel's People*. She'd done my makeup on the show and my wardrobe at the Emmys, and was always the first person I'd see in the morning and the last at night. Part of her job is to get everybody in a good psychological place before they gathered on the set, and she was terrific at it. She was always in good spirits, and it was infectious. She wore her heart on her sleeve, and it was difficult not to reciprocate with her. That and the fact that she made me look my very best, knew how to shade my nose and highlight my eyes in ways I'd never discovered before, made her something more than just a member of the crew.

"Are you okay?" she asked me, though it was obvious I was not.

I reached for composure.

"I'm just having my period. Everything's a lot worse when I'm bleeding."

"Tell me about it," she said. "It must be the moon; it's my time, too, and I'm ready to bite the next dog that barks at me."

I smiled, but I knew she saw my lip quivering. I told you I was a shitty actress.

"Are you and James okay?" Jesus, how obvious could I possibly be? More tears came, and I shook my head.

"When's the last time you went out dancing?"

I couldn't remember, and I told her so.

"Well, then, tonight's the night. Let's get you home and showered and all dolled up, and let's make 'em drool over us, what do you say?"

"No," I told her, "I'm really not up to it tonight."

"Sorry, Ms. Willoughby. I don't take no for an answer. We're going out and having a good time tonight. I'll take you home, help you look even more beautiful, and then we'll go out and break some hearts. We'll come back for your car later. Okay?"

What could I tell her, especially if she wouldn't take no for an answer?

FOUR

The drive west was even worse than the drive east had been, Interstate 10 a dismal blacktop inferno bisecting the bowel end of California. Traffic, seemingly mostly made up of giant trucks that trundled along at half the speed limit, blocked that bowel like a deep dish pizza, and for some reason, vehicular accidents bloomed in season.

On this trip, however, I was not alone. It might have been foolish to turn on the radio, but I could not take the solitary loneliness of the road any longer. CNN talked to me all across the desert; thanks to a Sirius subscription, I did not have to jump from local station to local station, and I could steer clear of the likes of blowhards like Rush Limbaugh, who seem to have laid claim to all stations across the AM dial. But the news was not cheery; the death of my wife had crept out into the media's bloodstream, growing more thunderous as the day wore on. My iPhone, cradled in its cup holder, buzzed and danced, begging for conversation from unrecognized numbers. The morning bloviators wept crocodile tears over the violent death not only of my wife, but of a nation's childhood. The innocence of beauty had been torn asunder by a mindless maniac and his bloodlust, leaving the corpse of a crumbling society soaked in its blood.

The News, its antennae vibrating as always to the tones of celebrity slaughter, missing Michael and Farrah and their too-soon-deceased like, had grown erect on Chase's death and its cautionary tale. They saw her as the chipper, chittering, pre-teen playmate of America. We'd grown up with her, loved her, shared the pain of her exploitation by her horndog producer and the resultant cast-aside fetus. They spoke of a woman unfamiliar to me, when it should have been me telling them all about who she was.

But no. I could have turned off the radio, or at least tuned it to a music station, but as I felt complicit in the death of my wife, at least psychically, I took the electronic tongue-lashing as my own personal punishment.

Hardy had been honest with me about the slaughter of my wife, but only to a certain point. The details of her murder were even more horrendous than those related to me. The more personal details of her murder—the missing strips of her skin from her back, the heart pattern shaved into the back of her scalp—were so far removed from the woman I lived with, the woman I had once adored and explored in intimate detail that it was difficult to reconcile them with Chase. The radio was talking about a case on *CSI*, not about the woman with whom I'd shared the last four or five years. This was a tale for the great unwashed, entertainment for the blood lust of the *hoi polloi*. Ratings.

Perhaps the cancellation of *Frankel's People* had been a mite hasty.

Ω Ω Ω

My eyes were filled with the grit of sleeplessness, my skull throbbing with voodoo jungle drum pain, my stomach so empty that its digestive juices worked on its own lining. I wanted Chase back. I wanted her sweet and beautiful and loving and sanguinary and voluptuous all over again. I would not scorn her again, I vowed to the skies, knowing I could never be held accountable. I would do what I could to love and support her, and deserve her love in return.

Big fucking deal, right? A lot of good my word ever meant to anyone, least of all to Chase. If there were such a thing as reincarnation, maybe I'd get a chance to do my penance and work my way up the evolutionary ladder. But more likely, I would merely spend the rest of my life in miserable servitude, then take the route from ashes to ashes, dust to dust.

Ω Ω Ω

I pulled over at a dusky little Mexican place on the sandy end of Indio right off the freeway. It was a low and squat little white stucco place, far removed from the snooty pavilions that lined the exclusive Country Club Drive a couple miles south. This place was working class; nary a Benz in the lot. My eyes had to adjust when I entered the gloomy little eatery, which was bedecked in sombreros and tiny, twinkling strings of multi-colored Christmas lights. There were WPA-era paintings of saguaro cactus and sleeping vaqueros and gloriously voluptuous wenches and stridently manly bullfighters on the walls, which were otherwise a drab sandstone color, smudged with decades of palm oil on the edges.

Soccer played silently on the TV set that hovered near the low ceiling in the corner. There were no other customers, it being between the assumed breakfast and lunch rush, so the waitress, who I guessed had been very pretty a couple of decades ago, and still moved with the carriage of a beautiful woman, smiled as she told me to sit anywhere I wanted. Her smile was unforced, genuine. I had none to return.

I sat in a corner in the windowless room, which was frigid; the air conditioner was stuck on high. The cold breeze felt good, and I let it caress me before I ordered a Mexican breakfast. The cathode ray magnet drew my eyes to its screen, even though I have neither knowledge nor interest in sports of any kind. Even though the volume was low, the excited Spanish chatter of the play-by-play filled the room.

The waitress, seeing that the game was getting under my skin, picked up the remote and started flipping through the channels until she stopped on Univision *Noticias*, where a lovely newscaster was telling the Latin world all about my wife's demise. There was breathless video of the motel room, with loving close-ups of the blood on the bed and the walls. There were clips, replete with laugh track, of the nymphet who had launched so many nocturnal emissions, being adorable and wise beyond her years. Nobody seemed to understand that this was a character, written by middle-aged men, portrayed by a little girl who found herself moved from a dairy farm outside of Bakersfield to a soundstage in Studio City, another in a long line of precocious innocents growing up under the tutelage of a studio teacher and hungry, predatory Hollywood heavyweights.

I remembered the girl I married. Her guard rarely came down, but when it did, when she exposed the bright, slightly sarcastic and wounded young woman, in those long-distant moments when she trusted me enough to reveal her creamy white filling, she had been sweet. And then, sour.

The television showed a montage video of moments in Chase's life, including a shot of our wedding in Palm Springs, just down the road from this little taco hacienda. I was struck by how genuine our smiles were at that impromptu little ceremony, and by how radiant Chase was in simple white lace and a veil. The waitress, who seemed held in thrall by the news, audibly gasped, and her hand fluttered to her chest like a wounded dove. She looked at me, her eyes now glassy, and pointed at the TV.

"Is that you?"

I just nodded, and she told me over and over how sorry she was. All I could do was breathe.

When she brought my chilaquiles and beans, all I could do was stare at them. I took some sips of the ice water, but that was all I could take in. Christina's powerful coffee had left its memory in my protesting stomach. The waitress was perceptive enough to turn off the TV and go back behind the cash register, pretending to be busy and giving me my privacy. But that just made this empty little café even lonelier. Sitting in the dim glow of twinkling holiday lights, I took a bite of the chilaquiles and tried to keep it down. There wasn't room for anything but regret inside me, so I threw a twenty-dollar bill on the table and took my leave.

Ω Ω Ω

The ride home was excruciating once I got past the 15, bumper-to-bumper under a scrim of orange pollution and ninety-five degree heat. All six lanes of the freeway, even the Diamond Lane, were slower than a Russian Oscar contender, jammed to capacity with angry Angelinos. All I wanted was to be home, out of the car, off this fucking endless freeway, and back in my bed, the place where this nightmare had begun. With luck, I'd awaken to a new morning, find that it had all been a dream, and go right down to Chase's room and tell her I'm sorry. But luck and I have never met. Luck is for, well, the lucky. So here I sat, ignoring the belligerent iPhone as it filled with pleading voice messages. I needed not to be driving; I needed to sleep; I needed to beg Chase's forgiveness.

Ω Ω Ω

There may be no place like home, but that's not necessarily a good thing. When I arrived, the news trucks surrounded my house like Conestoga wagons. A forest of portable antenna towers reached high, and the little cul-de-sac was a warren of video cameras and directional microphones. My first temptation was to turn right around, but where the fuck was I supposed to go? The tidy lawn was filled with media interlopers and curious bystanding gawkers crowding one another to get a closer look at I don't know what.

Instead, I nudged my car through the audience throng, forcing my way into the driveway. The ghouls descended, pressing their greasy little paws and faces up against the windows, leaving smeary prints all over the glass. I pushed the button to open the garage, and I was astounded by the *cojones* displayed by the handful that tried to enter the garage with me. Frazzled and outraged, I shouted at them that this was my property and to get the fuck out, hoping the door would squash them as it came tumbling down. The invaders backed away, and I stood alone in the hot, stuffy garage, reeling and wondering what to do. I opened the kitchen door and entered the house, locking the door behind me.

The first thing I did was to close all the shutters from the prying eyes and camera phones, feeling like I was blocking out the zombies in a George Romero movie. Late afternoon light still peeked in, but the gloom was palpable. Almost immediately, the doorbell rang. I tried to ignore it, but it was incessant. I could hear my name being shouted as if in a curse, and the telephone began wailing as well. Whoever was ringing the doorbell gave up and started pounding on the door, a sharp knock at first, but giving way to a heavy-fisted pounding. The shouts became more insistent. I silently cried uncle, and made my way to the front door and opened it.

Two men in dark, anonymous suits from Sears stood closest, with a famished pack of wolves clawing up from behind them. Microphones tried to reach around and past them, but they stood their ground, looking authoritative and immobile. One was white and the other black, but their size and features were nearly identical. Their faces were bland, and I'd never be able to pick them out in a crowd if I ever saw them a second time.

"We've been trying to reach you, Mr. Turrentine."

I felt like I was in trouble with the principal.

"Donald Freemantle and Eric Press, Federal Bureau of Investigation. May we come in?"

I knew I looked as thrashed as I felt, and was clearly not in the mood for visitors, but it wasn't like I had to make them coffee or anything. And I knew I'd have to talk to them sooner or later.

"Of course," I replied, and looked into the ravening hordes beyond them. "Any way you can help me get rid of... *them*?"

"Well, you have every right to order them off of your private property. Or..." He tried not to smile as he continued; "You could turn on the lawn sprinklers."

Naturally, I chose the latter, and my uninvited guests quickly evacuated the front lawn, hovering just beyond the reach of the rainbow water show.

Freemantle and Press entered the house and stood in front of the couch, waiting for me to give them permission to sit. It took me a moment; my social graces were still in hibernation. They sat, and I took the old Stickley chair across from them.

The men were very officious. I'd heard that the FBI recruited primarily from Mormons, and I could imagine each of these guys riding bicycles in their white shirts and ties in their formative teen years, going door to door and peddling the Word.

"First of all, let me offer our deep sympathy for the loss of your wife," Freemantle—or Press—said in a soft, sincere voice. I thanked him.

"Your wife was killed across the state line in Arizona, which makes it a Federal crime, hence our presence."

Well, I've written a couple of lawyer and detective episodes in my day, and I didn't realize that was the case. But my legal education had been conducted entirely at the University of Google, so I had to take their word for it.

"I understand."

"Mind if we record this?"

Did I? Yeah, kinda. But I certainly didn't want to seem defensive. So… "Of course not."

"Thank you." The black one, Press, I think, took out one of those little Flip HD cameras from his shirt pocket, snapped it on, and aimed it at me.

"Where were you last night, Mr. Turrentine?" Freemantle asked.

"I was at a screening at the TV Academy, then came home and went to bed. The Sheriff in Arizona called and woke me here to give me the news of my wife's death." My voice cracked, turning the final word into two syllables. It was starting to hurt. I glanced up over their shoulders at the density of objects on display around the living room, and realized that this was Chase's house, not mine. Every bit of its considerable decoration was hers; she had spent the first couple of years filling it with eccentric oddities that somehow worked, turned a simple little domicile into a home that reflected her personality. I just agreed with all of her choices because I didn't really care, though I knew that the house had become something really special. She was an artist, and our home reflected her creative choices, not mine. I just lived here.

"I'm sorry if this is painful for you, Mr. Turrentine, but we promise not to take too much of your time," Freemantle continued.

I just nodded, remembering the trip to New Mexico where she found the old saddle that sat by the fireplace.

"Why didn't your wife go with you?"

I looked back at him, realizing that there was a good chance I was under suspicion after all. I felt defensive.

"It wasn't her kind of thing. This was a pilot that a friend of mine produced, and she really didn't know him or care to see the show."

"Do you know what she planned on doing last night instead?"

"I assumed she was going to stay home and paint or something."

Press's face was as blank and expressionless as an Abercrombie and Fitch model's. The camera he held trained on me was starting to make me uncomfortable.

"Do you have any idea where she might have gone last night? Or how she ended up in Arizona?"

"I do not," I answered honestly. "I wish I did."

"Would you say you and your wife were happily married?"

How the hell do you answer something like that? Honesty seemed not to be the best policy here. Our marriage was only defined as such by a paper at the bottom of a drawer somewhere. *Happy* wasn't a word I'd considered in quite a while, in *any* context. Press kept watching me from the screen of his Flip.

"Well, we've had our problems, like any marriage, but I'd say yes." We *were* once, sure.

"What kind of problems?"

I started to sweat. I felt the hot breath of Chase's anger huffing against the back of my neck. As the two men stared at me with serene, unblinking, expectant faces, waiting for my answer, my heart rate accelerated.

"Well, you know, we've been going through a little rough spot for a while, and things have been, just, you know, a little, um, edgy, I guess."

The two men glanced at one another, and I swear Freemantle threw the trace of a smile at his partner. My throat went dry, but no matter how much I tried to clear it, the mucus remained stubbornly in place. I was sure now; I could tell that Press was doing his best to hide his joy at my discomfort. But they just silently stared at me, letting me squirm in the scythe of their purview. And that accusatory little Flip glared at me, daring me to claim my innocence. I refused to fill the guilty silence.

"What do you mean, 'edgy'?"

"You know, the business is in a pretty bad place right now, and it's taken a toll on both of us. Neither of us is where we want to be in our careers right now. And I guess maybe we kind of took it out on each other." That certainly was true, as far as it went.

"Did you kill your wife, Mr. Turrentine?"

"*Of course not!* " The outrage was genuine, but probably didn't play that way to the camera. "I was here in LA when she was killed! I just got back here from seeing her body in Arizona!"

"Did you have her killed?"

"Are you crazy?" I said, probably sounding like William Shatner on the 911 call when he phoned in the death of his wife.

They just looked at me, placidly awaiting an answer.

"Did you?"

"No!" I proclaimed.

Something about this didn't seem right. Again, I don't know much about the law, but what the fuck were the FBI doing here on the first day after a murder that took place in Arizona? They seemed to be enjoying my uneasiness way too much for by-the-book Feds.

"Can I see your ID?" I asked them.

"Do you have something to hide, Mr. Turrentine?"

These guys weren't FBI; more likely, they were TMZ.

"Let me see your ID!"

Press, or whatever his real name was, kept that damned Flip running, extending his arm to get it right up into my face.

"Get out of my fucking house!" I yelled, and they stood, backing away as I shoved them. I grabbed for the Flip, but Press anticipated me and yanked it away, keeping it running. I charged them and Press tumbled over Freemantle, and the Flip went flying. We dove for it, and I grabbed it away, threw it to the floor, and stomped it like a rhinoceros putting out a fire. Both of them scrambled for it, but by the time they got their filthy mitts on it, it was in pieces.

"Hope you've got a great lawyer," Freemantle snarled as they stood up against me.

"You're trespassing on private property! Now get the fuck out!"

"You invited us in, remember?" Yeah, like inviting Count Dracula into your home so he could be free to suck your blood.

"Get out!"

They did. Without their fucking Flip.

Ω Ω Ω

The house was often still when I was alone in it, but this was the first time it really felt lonely. Remote news vans, having bled all the footage they were going to get, began to pull away, and the crowd receded with the setting sun. The little house grew quiet within and without, and I felt unimportant, an intruder, useless, undeserving of residence here. All around me were monuments to a beautiful slaughtered woman; I stood alone in a room that she had dressed, a living set that she had created and occupied. My contribution here was a big screen Pioneer plasma display, a couple of Blu-ray players, and cabinets filled with discs filled with somebody else's imagination. She chose the artful antique Mission cabinetry that contained them, painted the coral and turquoise walls, festooned the rough-hewn open beams with painted strands of ivy. Her presence was everywhere; mine was subsumed, internal, insignificant. Chase was the light that filled the room; I was the darkness that extinguished that light.

I had dreamed of a time when we could escape the noose of one another, when I could lift myself out of the *ennui* of rotting matrimony, when I could man up and offer her a ticket out of this wrestling cage. I knew that both of us—and thinking about it now, especially Chase—could bloom and take flight once we were free of the chains that bound us to one another.

Why had we not divorced, if things grew so awful? I wish I had an answer. It wasn't as if we fought that often; we mostly just kept out of one another's way. I suppose it just seemed like too much work. Just like *everything* seemed like too much work for the last couple of years. Getting out of bed was a daily ordeal. The treadmill in my little office out back called to me every day, but the thickening cobwebs of disuse muffled its cry. After my morning chai latte, I would dutifully fire up the iMac, the one with the biggest screen I could order, and go through the emails, scan the trades and resent the seven-figure deals being made by twenty-one-year-old writers on hundred-and-fifty-million-dollar comic book adaptations. My Facebook page needed attention to deal with the friend requests from another couple of fat, virginal *Slaughter* fans, and there were YouTube videos of alligators eating water buffalo and puppies singing "Happy Birthday" that had to be acknowledged. And then, of course, it would be time for lunch.

There just didn't seem to be much time to deal with my marriage. We'd get around to that. We'd either fix it or end it, and the latter seemed far more likely… and far less work. One way or another, we'd take care of it.

But we didn't. Somebody else did it for us.

The gravity of Chase's murder was descending on me now, alone in the cheerful cacophony of design she left in her wake, though her cheer had been kept from me for some time. I wondered if she had smiled with friends when she was away from me. And then I wondered how long it had been since I'd even *had* any real friends. As the framed paintings and posters and the carved wooden lady salvaged from the prow of an old Mexican boat smiled down on me, as the hanging Balinese dolls and German marionettes hung frozen in their happiness, as the kitschy stuffed animals and carnival dolls danced in poses inspired by Chase, I couldn't even cry.

I walked to the counter and the answering machine was blinking the double zeroes of "memory full". I held my finger above the Play button for a full minute before I depressed it, only to unleash a torrent of eager reporters and a handful of acquaintances offering their sorrow. Chase's family had been killed in a car wreck a few years ago, and I'd had nothing to do with mine since I left home at sixteen, so there were no blood relatives on the line. There was a message from Chase's agent, one from mine, and another from our lawyer and business manager. That was about as intimate as it got. I erased them all, unplugged the hard line, and went upstairs to bed. This time, sleep was eager to claim me.

Ω Ω Ω

Since I had fallen asleep long before the sun had even set, I woke when it rose. Even so, it was a long night, even without the Ambien. But I had to pee like a racehorse. I relieved myself, staring in the reflection that watched me from the mirror above the toilet. I had to look away. Then, suddenly overwhelmed by an urgent rush of nausea, I threw up.

Disgusted, I flushed, threw on my morning sweats, and made my way downstairs with a new purpose.

I needed to know who killed my wife, and why.

Morning sun had a completely different effect than the ebbing sun of the afternoon. It did its best to inject cheer, making the place take on an actual glow, as if burnished. But the gloom was doing its best to overcome the light. I tentatively approached Chase's bedroom and eased open the door.

The room wasn't exactly messy, but it looked lived-in. The bed was still not made, and a T-shirt and running shorts were still damp with the musk of her sweat as they lay in a despondent heap on the floor. I picked them up and held them to my face, taking a deep breath, drawing Chase's scent deep into my own body. I sat on the bed and touched the sheets, which had gone cold in the air-conditioning. I picked up the pillow, and her scent mingled with a light perfume of vanilla and rose. It had been a long time since I'd stepped into this room, or even felt welcome here. It felt as though I was being naughty by being here, that I was going to get in trouble. I felt ten years old.

I lay back on her bed and closed my eyes, and could practically feel the gentle breeze of her breath. My skin erupted with gooseflesh as her ghost stroked my face.

My eyes flashed open, and it was just the flap of her pillowcase falling against my cheek.

I didn't belong in this room; I didn't deserve to be here. So I left and went to the kitchen.

I put on a kettle and surfed to the *LA Times* website. After the crowd that greeted my arrival home the previous day, it was surprising that the story wasn't even in the first section, but saved for the front of the local news. It had much bigger placement on the *VARIETY* site—"Moppet Topper Stopped by Slasher!"—with the *Hollywood Reporter* joining in the chorus. But it was the lead story on Yahoo!, Google, and all the other home pages. Video of my home was linked everywhere, and the number one YouTube video was the final episode of *The Crazy Frazees,* the one with the bikini. Today was a shining beacon of reportage.

I looked over at the telephone sitting silently on the counter. As the teapot began to sing, I went over and, after long moments of indecision, plugged it in. Almost immediately, it began to ring. I looked down at the caller I.D.: *LAPD* I knew I should answer it.

"Is this James Turrentine?"

"Yes."

"Did your wife drive a 2009 Toyota Prius?"

"2008."

"It's been found in the parking lot at Wilacre Park over at Franklin Canyon."

"Off Laurel Canyon?"

"Exactly."

"I'll be right there."

He started to say something, but I didn't stick around long enough to hear it.

FIVE

It was barely eight o'clock in the morning, but the San Fernando Valley was already starting to crisp in the dry summer heat. A dirty grey scrum obscured the mountains, and the Ventura Freeway was predictably jammed. It took me half an hour just to reach the 405, another twenty minutes to the Laurel Canyon turnoff. From there, I just had to eat shit and exhaust for another fifteen as I was caught in the cluster-fuck of the regularly employed headed over the hill to Hollywood.

When I finally pulled into the lot at Wilacre Park, the police were dusting the car for prints as it sat under the shade of sheltering oaks. I broke through the morning workout crowd that surrounded them, announcing my presence and presenting my spare key. The uniformed officer who took it from me was built like a fireplug: short and squat with a shaved head and an empty hole in his left earlobe. He wasn't fat, exactly, though his dark blue shirt struggled a bit at the buttons, and he had a bit of muffin-top action going on over his holster. I could see just the top of some Japanese characters tattooed to the back of his neck, peeking over the top of his dampening collar. Perspiration was already pooling at his armpits.

"Thanks for this, Mr. Turrentine," he told me as he took the key and unlocked Chase's royal blue Prius. "Looks like the car was left here last night, and was reported here in the morning. The park closes at dusk, and it's not legal to park here overnight, so when it was called in to us this morning, we ran the plates and found out that it belonged to your, uh, late wife."

I nodded, watching the slim, feminine handprints magically taking shape on the car door and window as they were dusted with carbon powder. There was no question that they belonged to Chase. She had lovely hands with long, tapered fingers, slender to the point of delicacy.

"Sorry. Officer Demetrious." He reached out and shook my hand, even though he wore latex gloves. "Arizona Sheriff's called in, and we're doing them the courtesy of lifting prints for their investigation. I'm very sorry about your loss, sir."

"Thank you."

He stepped over and reached for the car door, then stopped and looked at me. "You mind?"

"Of course not."

He opened the door and it sighed a cool breath into the August heat. I looked inside and was not surprised to find it fastidiously tidy. Aside from a bottle of water and a copy of a book called *The Highly Sensitive Person*, the car was as barren as if it had just left the showroom floor. I noticed the ring of lipstick around the sports cap on the water bottle and realized that it had come from Chase's mouth. I hated to think that it had been her final kiss.

Another officer was dusting the passenger side of the car. The gathering crowd was an interesting mix of grey-haired organic types in sagging tie-dyed T-shirts, perfectly sculpted tight young actors with shaved chests and legs, former soap stars hiding behind giant sunglasses, beautiful but aging women with six-pack abs and robust augmented breasts barely haltered in stretchy sports bras, a school gym class, grotesquely overweight women with their Chihuahuas hell-bent for the *Biggest Loser* tryouts, and the occasional dog walker with her gaggle of golden retrievers, Italian greyhounds, boxers, and Yorkies, each seemingly eager for a taste of human flesh.

I watched in fascination as Demetrious laid thick strips of clear, sticky tape across the carbon powder to lift the prints before he pressed them onto blank white pages in a book. He probed the car for fibers, pulling up a strand or two of long, glossy black hair: obviously Chase's.

"Anything on your side, Tony?" he asked the skinny Latino cop behind the paintbrush full of grey powder.

"It's clean," Tony answered, to nobody's surprise.

Demetrious held out the book of prints to show me. "These appear to be all from the same person. I'm guessing your wife."

"Looks like her hands," I replied.

"We'll run them anyway, just to be sure."

"Great, thank you," was the best I could muster.

"I think we've got everything we need here, sir. Would you like an officer to take your wife's car home?"

"Would you do that?"

"Of course."

"You got a pen? I'll write down the address."

"That's okay; we know where it is."

"Could you just put the key through the mail slot on the door?"

"Glad to, sir."

Everybody was being so nice and California-polite; it unnerved me. "Thank you," I offered.

"That's our motto: to protect and serve." He turned to his partner. "Tony, could you drive the car to Mr. Turrentine's residence?" Tony returned the request with a mock salute, and Demetrious handed over the key to him. And that was it. Tony hopped in the car, threw me a smile, and pulled out of the parking lot in my wife's car.

"You have a nice day, sir," Demetrious said before he hopped into his marked cruiser and made his way out of the lot. I stared after him, incredulous. Have a nice day? I mean, really, the day after my wife's been slaughtered, mutilated, virtually hacked and slashed to pieces: *have a nice day?* If this were a *Law and Order* assignment, I could never have gotten away with such a civil, courteous exchange with the husband of a murdered TV star. And then, interview over. Hell, it had never even taken place.

I stood in the parking lot as the crowd started to disperse, again draped in the cloak of staring eyes. That was it? They found Chase's car, checked it for fingerprints and fibers, and split? Some investigation.

The shade of the towering oaks was a respite in the blooming morning heat. Even with the choking traffic of Laurel Canyon Boulevard just on the other side of a row of eucalyptus trees, the air smelled different here. I hadn't spent time outdoors in a long time; home was a cave where I slowly became a hermit, a typing misfit with little contact with the world outside. My friendships and associations were mostly virtual or electronic, my outings rare. It felt strange to be under a sky and not a roof, the scent of spruce needles baking in the heat of the sun.

I remembered feeling her dampness on the workout clothes I had found on the floor of her bedroom, and realized that she must have been running here, that this might have been the last place she'd been before her fatal journey to Arizona. I decided to retrace her steps.

The trail has a steep beginning, and I was winded from the time my hike had commenced. But the summer wildflowers embraced me, encouraged me to keep going. Avoiding the ubiquitous mines of dog shit, I made my way up the hill, wondering if Chase came here often. It's funny how little I knew about her life of late; as I hibernated in my cave, I assumed that she hibernated in hers. But this was a world far removed from her paintbrushes, from her career, this was outside, open, a little bit scary. Maybe it didn't intimidate her, but it was starting to frighten me. I kept climbing up and up, seeking some evidence of her presence, something that revealed her to me. She had been a secret, but over time, as we grew closer, more intimate, I learned the combination to her safe full of mystery. But as we used up our pleasure together, the door slammed tightly shut, and her secrets asserted themselves anew.

I was out of breath when I hit the peak of the trail, the half-way point that overlooks Coldwater Canyon with a breathless view. The San Fernando Valley was spread out before me, and I knew it was offering up its puzzles. If only I spoke its language.

Individual, interchangeable young women of an anonymous beauty jogged past me, and their amplified breasts didn't even bob; they had no relation to the physics of gravity. They all looked alike, as if there'd been a sale on those noses and lip jobs on Rodeo Drive this week. Chase had never been one of those. Once met, Chase was never forgotten. The little swoop of her nose was not a flaw; it made her more uniquely beautiful. One eye was a little bigger than the other, and it gave her an incredibly sexy little squint. No surgeon's blade had ever touched her skin; no color ever tinted her nearly raven hair, which usually just hung long and free and straight, a stranger to rollers and perms. Pretty poison, indeed.

I was winded, sweat drying in the arid breeze that kicked up dirt on the trail. A dust devil swirled toward me, then twisted around me, throwing me into the eye of this miniature hurricane. Grit filled my eyes and a brown cloud blinded me. Then, suddenly, it passed, a dervish that ran ferociously down the hill I had just traversed. I turned around and went back down in its wake, dust settling just before I trod in its path. There was nothing for me here, nothing but a decision. Since I drove her away, probably to her very death, I would avenge her murder. I would seek out its source, try to make things right. The clock would be turned back to a time when she needed me as much as I needed her right now. Chase, I swore to the whispering wind as it withered to a dusty breeze, I will honor your memory. I will be redeemed.

I thought I heard her voice laugh in the sky above.

Ω Ω Ω

We were homebodies, Chase and I, cave-dwelling artists who dimmed in the light of social intercourse. It was so even before our infatuation with one another had turned to enmity, but grew worse when we retired to our individual warrens. Chase went out more than I did; were there haunts that she frequented? I didn't even know. I had lost track of her life, and knew little of her time away from the house. So for now, at least, the only place I could think to go was home. So home I went.

The blue Prius sat in the driveway, safely and carefully delivered. The media, having already sucked whatever visual life it could from the home of the murdered television child star, had not returned to lick the bowl. A handful of civilians littered the sidewalk in front of the house, but as I pulled up, they maintained a respectful distance. I pulled around the Prius and into the garage, and entered directly into the kitchen and an empty, silent house.

This time, the archaic answering machine registered few calls. They were deletable, either reporters or strangers leaving weird and creepy messages, and I threw them all away, putting the machine back to zero. I picked up the phone and went back through screen after screen of caller I.D., just wondering if any of the names or numbers might provide a clue. All it provided was a headache. All I wanted were the calls that came in between the time I'd last seen my wife on Wednesday morning and the midnight hour of her death that night. But there were no calls at all at that time. What I really needed to see was her mobile phone, a more direct line to her life. I wondered where it was.

I went into her studio, and the walls were lined with her Primal Scream series of sketches and paintings. The rage and fury they expressed had never been so overt, so extreme as now, in the wake of her death. Faces howled in animal anguish as bodies split apart between devil-vs.-angel dualism. The wounds grew deeper on each canvas. They grew more colorful, too; the stack of canvases started with charcoal, monochromatic sketches, but she turned to oils, and the color palette grew more crimson with each attempt. The paint grew thicker, too, more three-dimensional, as if the art was created from the body's own offal. But there, off to the side, hidden behind the gathered objects of a projected still life, a simple painting lay against the wall. It was obviously a self-portrait, just a few minimalist strokes in blue paint: hair, wide, sad eyes, a hint of a nose, and no mouth at all. Its mute peace stood in bold contrast to the ferocious howls of the faces in all of the other works, and made it all the more disturbing.

Ω Ω Ω

I snapped out of a trance, finding myself standing in the middle of the living room for God knows how long. The house mocked me with Chase's presence. Seconds ticked past, leisurely and inevitable. The box of light from the living room window crept slowly across the floor, threatening to burn my feet.

What happened to you, Chase?

Where did you go?

Who did this to you?

And why?

I looked over to her bedroom and the open door that begged me to enter, and answered its call.

The room was filled with daylight, striking the hanging crystals and making a kaleidoscope of colors dance on the walls. Her workout clothes were still in a heap on the floor where I'd left them, but when I picked them up they were dry. There was a faint, salty crust outlining the armpits, but that was the only trace left of her now. I held them to my face and breathed deeply; the hint of her perspiration's tang was temporal, and dissipating quickly. I shook out the T-shirt and shorts, folded them, and draped them over the foot of the bed.

I slowly ran my hand over the rumpled bed, feeling the slight dip of where her body had lain, alone, night after night. I don't know why, but I decided to make her bed.

I pulled back the covers and fluffed the pillows, discovering myself caressing them as I carefully lay them in place. The pillowcase was very slightly discolored in the middle from the oil of her skin. I tried to smell her there, but none of her scent remained.

I began to smooth the bottom sheet... and something caught my eye.

It was tiny and barely noticeable as it lay against the off-white bamboo fiber sheet. But it was right there in the middle of the bed, coiled like a delicate copper spring: a red, curled pubic hair.

Chase's hair was a brown so dark it was nearly black. And besides that, she did the near-Brazilian thing; the only hair between her legs was a short little landing strip that pointed at her clitoris. As I stared at the nasty little curl, my mouth gaping in wonder, the late morning sun hit it and made it gleam.

My heart started to pound and my stomach curdled. Who was the red-haired scumbag who'd been fucking my wife?

And did the red-haired scumbag who'd been fucking my wife kill her, too?

I bent down and picked up the nasty little hair, holding it close to my face. It was surprisingly delicate, fine, almost fragile. I pulled a Kleenex from the box on the nightstand, gently folded it around the hair, and put it in my pocket.

Who did she know with red hair? For that matter, who did *I* know with red hair?

At that moment, the shock that my wife had taken a lover was almost as devastating as her murder. I was thunderstruck, flabbergasted, dumbfounded, all of those words that don't quite reach the level of nauseous astonishment that had me reeling.

I stormed out of her bedroom and into her studio, where her laptop stood open but sleeping next to a messy stack of papers on its antique Art Deco metal desk. With a brisk swipe of my finger across the trackpad, it woke to a cheery desktop photo of Chase holding a pair of snakes at the mouth of a cave at a Thai temple from a vacation we took on our first anniversary. I was notably absent in the shot.

Her address book opened with a simple click. It was a long list of names, mostly familiar, many not. They appeared to be primarily business-oriented: lots of network and studio names and numbers. Not a lot of personal ones, much like my own contact list. Those that I did not recognize meant nothing to me.

I bit my lower lip as I stared at her Mailbox. Even though she was no longer alive, it felt wrong to delve into her email correspondence. Her privacy, however, was no longer an issue. It was the only place that I could turn for clues to her murder, so I clicked, and it all opened up to me.

All of that nothing. EBay receipts, a couple of scripts from her agents, an ongoing chat with a gallery on La Cienega that was doing a show with art by celebrities. Nothing at all of a personal nature. Her Inbox was even more devoid of life than my own.

I opened her iPhoto files. Most of the pictures were from vacations we had taken, a big group of wedding pictures when we both wore smiles, on-set photos from *Frankel's People*, some gallery shoots, even a handful of arty nudes that I had shot right after we came back from Thailand. There were a few shots of Chase smiling with some groups of friends, but as the dates drew more recent, those shots were less frequent and filled with fewer faces.

Nary a redheaded stranger among them.

I closed the laptop, completely at sea.

The stack of papers beckoned me next, atypically slovenly for my somewhat anal-retentive bride. There were bills and scribbled notes and receipts on top of a lined yellow legal pad. Edges of a pencil sketch peeked out from under the detritus, so I pushed it aside. The drawing was mournful: a woman's face seeming to melt to the edge of the paper below her. It was sad, heartbreaking even; but when you looked closer, it was even worse. The lines that formed the drawing were letters, and they spelled out a single word:

Lonely.

From that moment on, the Hate tank registered empty.

Ω Ω Ω

There was a knock on the door, gentle, tentative, but I was glad for the distraction. I left Chase's fortress of solitude and opened the door to two familiar figures: my agent and hers. Their faces were pale, sympathetic, but not in a phony, Hollywood way. They stood in genuine sorrow as they asked if it was okay to come in.

Jerry Atherton represented me, though we hadn't had much to do for the last couple of years. But he was still doing what he could for a client stuck in neutral. He stood close to six-foot-five, but was thin and uncoordinated. The tailored suit tried to make up for his ungainliness, and almost succeeded; it surely cost multiple thousands, but the Swatch on his wrist kind of ruined the effect. Though not much over thirty, his hair was thinning rapidly. Theresa Black had been Chase's agent since the *Frazee* days. Her real name was Schwarzwald, but she'd simplified it when she'd had her nose bobbed and the lipo. She was sixtyish, her hair blonde frosted over black, neither hue with roots in reality. Her face was tight and her forehead shiny and immobile. Her hairline hadn't met her ears in a decade. If she measured five feet tall, she had to be in heels.

"We tried to call, but I'm sure the phone's been crazy for you," Theresa said in her *faux* British accent, taking a seat on the couch.

"This is terrible, Jimmy," Jerry said, laying a hand on my shoulder. "A real tragedy. We're so, so, sorry." Theresa nodded and her eyes started to tear. She took a handkerchief out of her purse and dabbed at her nose, sniffling. I had never seen her express an emotion before, other than greed.

Jerry opened a white paper bag and pulled out a big Starbucks cup. "I brought you a chai latte."

I thanked him and sat on the Stickley across from them. It moaned from the weight I'd put on since *Slaughter* was cancelled.

"Thanks for coming by," I said, my voice a croak. I hadn't been using it much of late.

"It's the least we could do, honestly," he said, and Theresa nodded in concurrence. "Are you okay? Is there anything we can do for you?"

"I'm shitty, but thanks for asking."

They looked at one another, maybe sorry they'd come after all. I regretted it right away.

"Sorry," I apologized, "but this has been a total shock. I went out to Arizona and saw her body, and… and…"

"You have nothing to apologize for, James. This is horrible, horrible…"

"Horrible," agreed Jerry. "Listen, I can have Janet take care of all of the funeral plans, if you want. You shouldn't have to worry about shit like that."

Funeral plans? I hadn't even thought about a funeral. I suddenly felt thirty pounds heavier.

"Thanks, Jerry."

"Really, no problem. Anything you need, you just let me know, okay?"

"Thanks."

"Or me," Theresa added, ever the competitor.

"Great. I will."

There was a long, awkward silence before Jerry spoke up again.

"Do they have any idea who did it?"

I shook my head. "Not that I know of. They said they'd call with any information."

"Horrible," Theresa added. "Just horrible."

Salome danced in my head again, and Chase's butchered face stared at me in angry accusation.

"He... he cut her up," I said, not to them or to anybody, I guess. "Bad."

"You shouldn't have seen that," Theresa admonished. "They should never have let you look at her that way. That's no way for a husband to remember his wife."

I shook my head. "I had to."

"Horrible," said Jerry. And then, more awkward silence.

"I'm going to find him," I said to myself. "I swear to God, I'm going to find him."

"Good for you, James," Jerry said.

They looked at one another, mystic knights of the Spectacular Artists Agency, bound in a secret handshake. They surely had more to discuss, but neither of them wanted to begin the conversation.

"Thanks for coming by," I said. "I really appreciate it."

"Sure, sure," Jerry said. "The least we could do."

"The very least," Theresa chimed it. But neither of them rose from the couch.

"You look good, Jimmy," said Jerry, "considering."

"I look like shit and feel like shit. But thanks, Jerry. I appreciate your concern." I stood up, hoping to encourage their departure.

"Anything you need, Jimmy, you hear me? Anything."

"Thanks, Jerry. Theresa."

They still wouldn't get up off the couch.

"All right, I'll take it," Theresa spat, shaking her head in disgust at Jerry. "There's one other thing. I know this is a terrible time to discuss business, but this is something that's just come up, and it's something we have to talk to you about now."

The phone started to ring; it was from the La Paz Sheriff's Department.

"Excuse me a second," I told them, then answered the phone. It was Hardy. I held up my hand.

"Mr. Turrentine?" Blah, blah, blah. Niceties. Cut to the chase, okay? I'm busy with my misery.

"I just wanted to check in with you, bring you up to date a little. We haven't recovered any evidence that might lead us to a suspect yet; no weapon, no fingerprints, no witnesses, no unaccounted for excretions or fluids." He was very matter-of-fact, but more gentle than officious. Human, even.

"Thanks, Sheriff. I appreciate your keeping me informed."

"Listen," he continued. "We're coming to LA tomorrow to continue the investigation, and we'd like to spend a little time with you, if that's okay."

"If that's okay?"

He chuckled. "Well, whether it's okay or not. Busted."

"It's okay," I told him. "I'll be here."

"We can probably be there around lunchtime. Not a big deal, just the usual questions, check your wife's belongings, things like that."

Murder investigations were much more polite than I'd imagined.

"Fine."

"Great. See you then." He hung up, and I was back with the Terrors of Tinseltown. They looked at me expectantly, so I fulfilled their expectations. "That was the Sheriff in charge of the investigation in Arizona."

"Any news?" Jerry asked.

"Nothing."

"Just horrible," Theresa said.

This was getting tiresome. "So you were saying?" Or *not* saying...

"Right." Theresa gave her nose another wipe.

"Bravo has come to us with a proposal. They want to document the investigation into your wife's murder, ride-alongs, forensics labs, witness interviews, the whole magilla. They've got Anthony Pellicano and his team on board, and they'll guarantee thirteen episodes, with an option for another thirteen, should the continuing investigation merit it. John Walsh has given a tentative yes to hosting, and you'll get EP credit, twenty grand an episode, doubling the total if the murderer is caught as the result of our investigation, triple if he's caught while cameras are rolling."

I just stared at them, my mouth in a Neanderthal gape, my eyes unblinking.

"I know, I know, it's absolutely tasteless. Disgusting." Theresa's face took on a disgusted sneer, as if this was all of a sudden way too tawdry to even discuss. "But as your representatives, it's our duty to convey this to you."

"It's a pretty sweet deal, really, Jim," Jerry said. "I know times have been tough for you lately, and it's a way to put that behind you."

"And it's a way to get the full weight of one of the finest private security companies in the world in on the investigation," Theresa added eagerly. "Do you really think some hick Arizona sheriff is going to solve this? These are some of the top criminal minds working!"

Now Jerry started to get excited. "The working title is *Cut to the Chase: Avenging the Child Star Angel*. But if you don't like it, you come up with your own. You're the creative one, and you have full title approval."

"The Bravo brass are very high on this. And they feel it's got huge international potential, and that's a whole other pot." Theresa was practically licking her fingers. "And I think I can get them up to twenty-five per."

"And it's Bravo! *Housewives* is starting to sag, and they think this can be their next big show!"

They sat there panting like eager contestants on The Dating Game. I just stared at them, incredulous, for long, silent moments.

"What do you think, Jim?" Jerry asked.

What did I think?

Yes, my marriage to Chase had withered into disaster. We couldn't be in each other's presence without a war of words, or, worse, a journey to the silent ice planet. But I had seen her beauty hacked away by a madman's knife, her blood spattered against the walls, the rusty scent of her death permanently etched in my nose.

I stood up above them, and they looked up with eager, expectant smiles.

"What do I think?"

"That's what we're here for," Jerry answered.

"I think *fuck you!*"

I yanked them up out of the couch and shoved them violently to the door.

"I think you are the slimiest, greediest, ugliest fucking scumbags I've ever seen! Chase's death is not for sale! Get the fuck out of my house, you fucking insects, you talentless, parasitic, bloodsucking, money-grubbing, planet-spoiling, lame fucking excuses for humans!" As a writer, I wish I'd been more eloquent, my invective more annihilating, but it was the best I could come up with at the time.

I shoved them hard against the wall, and Theresa tumbled over her Loeffler Randalls. The look she aimed at me was pure hatred.

"You fucking hypocrite! I know what was going on with you and Chase. You didn't even *like* her! And she felt the same about you! It wouldn't surprise me if *you're* the one who killed her!"

I threw open the door.

"I said get the fuck out of my house!" I shoved them out.

"*Chase's* house!" Theresa spat as I slammed the door in their wake. I stood with my back against the door for a long time, begging Chase's forgiveness.

Joni Mitchell was right: you don't know what you've got 'til it's gone.

Ω Ω Ω

I walked to the picture window and watched them leave. They drove off together in Theresa's Mercedes. She slammed into the mailbox on the way out of the driveway, knocking it to the ground before she peeled away in embarrassment... if an agent is capable of being embarrassed.

Chase's Prius sat alone in the driveway; it was time to put it away. I saw the key, still on the floor in front of the front door, where the LA cop had dropped it through the mail slot, picked it up and went outside. As I strode the rock path under the canopy of roses, the postman came walking to the end of the cul-de-sac, his heavy bag of mail over his shoulder. He was in his summer togs, long legs with bony knees trailing from his Government Issue grey shorts, sweltering under his USPS safari helmet. He stared at the collapsed mailbox, then at the stack of mail in his hands.

I went over to him. "I'll take it," I offered, and he looked up, and jumped with a start.

"Thanks," he stuttered, not quite sure what to say. I hadn't seen him before on this route, but Chase was the one who always picked up the mail, so I wasn't sure if he was new or not. I took the stack of correspondence from him, and he was sweating profusely in the Woodland Hills summer heat.

"I... I'm sorry for your loss, Mr. Turrentine," he offered from beneath his sunglasses.

"Thank you," I answered. He stood there, not knowing the proper etiquette. I guess he was waiting to be dismissed. "I appreciate it," I hinted.

He lifted the helmet and wiped his brow with the back of his arm, then ran his fingers through his long, thick, wet, wavy red hair that fell around his face in angelic ringlets.

"Okay, then," he said. "Guess I'd better get going." I must have gaped, as he squirmed under my stare. All I could see was the hair, the red hair, the crimson halo, the copper mane. It flared like a dying flame in the sunlight. The rest of the frame around him had been erased.

"What's your name?" I asked him.

"Wesley. Wesley Malone."

"A good Irish name."

"I guess so."

"They call you Red?"

"There's some I let call me Red. But not without an invitation."

"Did my wife call you Red?"

"Sorry?"

"Chase. Did she call you Red? Did she get your invitation?"

"I don't understand." Yeah, I'll bet he didn't.

"Yes you do. You understand perfectly, don't you?" I pulled his hat away and threw it across the lawn.

"What did you do that for?"

"I asked you a question!"

He walked across the lawn toward the hat, but I kicked it away from him, grabbed it and held it to my chest, like a nine-year-old playing keep-away. His pale, almost opalescent skin was pinking on its way to match his fiery locks.

"What's the matter with you?"

Suddenly furious, I sent the hat sailing with all my might, a jungle Frisbee taking flight like an Ed Wood UFO.

I ran up to him and grabbed his shirt in both hands, yanking him face-to-quavering-face like I was channeling Bruce Willis or something. Jesus, I would never have written a scene like this. But I was out of control, practically rabid; I could feel projectile saliva being flung with each crazy word.

"Did you fuck my wife?"

"What?"

I pulled him even closer. He'd had a hot dog with sauerkraut already today. "You heard me! I said, *did you fuck my wife?*"

The disbelief and consternation that overtook his expression brought it suddenly to a close.

"You're fucking crazy, man. I've never fucked anybody's wife."

The obvious innocence of this gawky, fresh-faced kid with the cherry Jesus crown put out my fire, and it was time for my face to flush, with a shame I could not hide. The tough guy I wore fell away, and I was once again a failed TV writer, creeping painfully past thirty with a softening middle and a dead wife that everybody wanted a piece of.

I let go of his shirt, and wrapped my arms around him in a hug, which understandably made him squirm.

"I'm sorry, man," I said into his shoulder. "Chase is dead, and I'm going a little crazy."

He gently peeled out of my embrace, and I was glad he hadn't chosen to put the dog repellent to use.

"I get it, dude, it's okay. I'm really sorry." He was being more of a mensch than I would have under the same circumstances. "We all go a little crazy sometimes."

Shit, even the mailmen spoke in Hitchcock references in LA.

"I'm gonna go now," he said as he slowly, cautiously backed away from me, "okay?"

I nodded, apologetically raised my hands, letting him know everything was cool. His image rippled in the water pooling in my eyes.

"I'm really sorry," I repeated, because I really was. A quick look around the cul-de-sac showed faces watching from behind the neighborhood windows, and closing blinds and curtains as our eyes met. I quickly made my way to Chase's car and climbed inside. The garage door opened at the push of a button, and I coasted in on silent electric power, closing the door behind me.

I sat in the gloom of the silent garage, thinking about what an asshole I was.

SIX

It always comes down to sex, doesn't it?

I'm not a Freudian or anything, but it does seem to be the primary motivator for all human interaction, right? We begin our lives with an orgasm—hopefully two—from happy zygote to a trip down Mama's birth canal. From the suckling of the teat to mating for life, if such a thing is possible, we live our lives orally, carnally, physically. Yeah, maybe a kiss is just a kiss, but for me, it used to mean something.

I was an only child, and though I felt love from my parents, it seemed delivered at a distance, politely, without much physical expression. I think my parents were uncomfortable with such intimacy, even between themselves. To this day, I still remember a time when I couldn't have been more than five or six, sitting on my father's lap as he watched cartoons with me. I don't know why, but I just felt overwhelmed with feeling for him, and hugged him and gave him a big kiss, right on the mouth. Rather than return the kiss, he seemed to get angry with me. I felt a hardness forming in his lap, and he quickly lifted me up and sat me on the floor. He looked like he wanted to spank me, and I wondered what I had done wrong. I just felt that swelling of love that a daughter had for her daddy, and it got me in trouble. I withheld those feelings after that; I thought that they were bad.

It was not a huggy, kissy, feely kind of a family; my parents showed their love in other ways. They indulged me, but I'd like to think they didn't spoil me. We didn't have a lot of money, and Bakersfield wasn't the kind of place where you dream about Prada and Mercedes, but I got most of what I needed, if not everything that I wanted. And that was good enough. I didn't really want all that much, anyway.

It was a funny feeling, right around the time I started middle school, when people started to treat me differently, let me move to the front of the line, gave me their desserts at lunchtime, wanted to be my friend. Boys would either punch me or kiss me; I never knew which to expect. But I grew to learn that they both meant the same thing.

So when my mother drove me down to Hollywood for an open casting call for *The Crazy Frazees*, it was a shock to be ushered into a waiting room filled with pretty little girls who were just like me. But most of them had makeup on, and sexy clothes, and acted like they'd been here and done that a hundred times before. And none of them would talk to me… or each other, for that matter. They all seemed *mean*.

Maybe that's why I got the part; I hadn't learned to be mean yet. Well, that and my early development. I'm sure the tits on a tweener had a lot to do with it. Like I said, it's always sex. But this was my first ever audition, and I got the role. I had no idea how rare that was.

It's easy to see why actors can become raging egomaniacs. You get special treatment all the time, people want to be photographed with you, be around you, hope that some of what's special about you will rub off on them. They give you things, they call you beautiful, they don't let you do any of the physical work; there are people to do that for you. And later on, if you really care about acting, you have to be sensitive enough to portray the broadest range of emotions and insensitive enough to be judged and rejected almost every time you step into a casting office.

But the *Frazees* experience was like being in a new family together. And when Peter, a handsome, dashing man with swept-back hair that was silver on the sides, always dressed in a suit and tie, with teeth and a tan too perfect for nature, when he paid special attention to me, when he hugged me after a good take and left his hand lingering on my shoulder, I curled into its warmth. He told me how special I was, but it was private; he didn't want the other cast members to see that I was his favorite. He treated me like a grownup, and I blossomed as I began to feel like one. At fourteen.

And when the ultimate hymen-busting ritual finally took place—at night, in his office, after everyone had gone home— it started with dryness and pain, and ended in a shocking physical sensation I'd never felt before. Amid tears and wet spots, I fell in love with him, and knew that he loved me, too; he told me so on all of our subsequent secret nights together.

Then the periods stopped, and so did his attention. When I told him I thought I was pregnant, he sneaked me off to a friend of a friend, who performed the abortion in a Beverly Hills home theater, the better to keep this from the press. It hurt, and I bled and bled, and Peter's special affection ceased. And I never wanted to make love again.

I did, of course. Sometimes it even felt good.

But I didn't combust again until Jimmy, and even that eventually curdled. The fire burned brightly, leaving embers glowing in memory, if not in fact.

I knew what it was to be desired, but what I needed was to be wanted, to be loved. It was like that at first with James, but after the raging inferno or our first year or two, desires were slaked, the real world crept in, and the fire was put out.

Honestly, I didn't miss the sex all that much, and I don't think Jimmy did, either. What hurt was the loss of all of that feeling we'd shared after the walls came down. I returned to my lockbox, and hid the key under the mat.

Ω Ω Ω

So I said yes to Toni, in the pine-scented heat of the Wilacre Park parking lot. I resisted at first, feeling cloistered, introverted, solitary. But she was very convincing. Her smile and her enthusiasm and her very lightness charmed me, brought out a grin of my own that had lain fallow for way too long. You know what? I could stand having a night out surrounded by people and music and fun again. She laughed, clapped hurray, and gave me a big hug, then pulled me like a teenager over to her little convertible Mini, and pulled us out onto Laurel Canyon, blasting the Poppees on her car stereo. I felt a weight lift off my shoulders, and actually started to sing along, even though I didn't know the words.

Ω Ω Ω

I was surprised to see that James's behemoth Beemer was not at home when we pulled up. He was rarely away from the house. I felt better going inside without him there to harsh the new-found buzz. The sun was warming with breaths of hot wind and the little house welcoming, like a little slice of lemon pie begging to be eaten.

By the time we entered the house we were giggling like teenage girlfriends. I always love the reactions of people when they enter my home. It's been my project, my passion, to make a place that really welcomes you, makes you feel at home. It's cluttered with eclectic stuff: you know, dolls, antique little baby carriages, ancient Thai headdresses, elderly puppets and toys, turn-of-the-century stuffed animals, Art Deco copper ballerinas, old costume skirts spread onto the walls like tapestries, even a couple of my paintings hiding in the corners.

When Toni entered for the first time, she actually gasped, laughed and clapped her hands. People either loved the place or were silent when they first saw it, and Toni's delight made my day.

"Oh, Chase, what a beautiful place! Did you do this yourself?"

I probably blushed under the weight of her enthusiasm and told her yes.

"It's like out of a movie, some kind of fairy tale or something! I've never been any place like this!"

"You sure know how to say all the right things, don't you?"

She gave me a hug, like an excited little girl. I felt a little awkward, I mean, I didn't really know her all that well, but I hugged back.

"You want some iced tea or something?" I asked her as she inspected our little cottage.

"After you give me the grand tour," she said, taking my hand to be led from room to room. The house isn't exactly Disneyland or anything, but it held her in its thrall nonetheless. The tour didn't take long, as it really is a pretty tiny little place with not many rooms, but she loved it, and it really raised my spirits.

We ended up in the kitchen, and I poured us some iced green pomegranate tea. It tasted great after our summer hike, and I closed my eyes as I held the icy glass to my forehead.

"This is great!" Toni said. "Did you make this?"

"Trader Joe's," I answered. "Listen, make yourself comfortable. I've got to take a shower. I must smell like a football player."

"You smell great," she said. But I knew that wasn't true.

I gulped down the rest of the tea, rinsed my glass and put it in the sink.

"You didn't show me the bathroom."

She was right; I hadn't. "Come on."

I led her down the hall and opened the door. I knew she would love it. It was one of my favorite things about the house. The ground floor bathroom, *my* bathroom, was one of my pet projects. The sink, tub, and toilet were all Art Deco, sea-foam green ceramics. I'd done the floors and lower walls in black and maroon period tiles, and all of the fixtures were period chrome. I'd painted the walls with undersea scenes inspired by the murals in the Casino Theater on Catalina Island.

"Oh, my God," she breathed. "It looks like Catalina!"

"I can't believe you recognized it!"

"Are you kidding? It's gorgeous! Who did you get to paint it?"

Time for me to blush again. "I did it."

"Chase! Are you shitting me? It's awesome!"

I thanked her.

"God, I had no idea you were so talented!"

I was starting to drown in her praise. It was more than enough.

"I'm going to take a shower now; I don't think I can take any more compliments."

"I'm sorry, but you know I mean it, don't you?"

"Thanks, Toni. I'll just be a minute. Make yourself at home."

"Sure. Thanks."

She headed back into the living room, and I stepped into the bedroom and out of my stinky trail clothes. They were sopping wet.

The tiles were cool as I padded across the bathroom floor to the tub. It felt nice after the day's heat. I had to admit that my spirits had been raised. From the dead. Toni had really cheered me up, and as I looked around at the bathroom, I felt the sin of pride well up a bit.

A ripple of gooseflesh ran the length of my body as the air conditioning blew on me. I liked my shower lukewarm, but blasted the water at full force. I stepped under the 1920s waterfall showerhead, and tensions were washed away with the layers of sweat. I lathered up with the French verbena soap and closed my eyes. I actually started to feel like going dancing again. I hadn't done that in a couple of years, and frankly, had never really understood the attraction. I don't know; I guess I've got the music in me, after all. That was a surprise.

As I luxuriated, I heard Toni turn on the stereo. It must have been my New Age Pandora station, gentle, light, not really "music", but it put me at ease. I thought she'd change it to something more her style, but she just left it there and turned it up a little. Andes pipes or something. It was nice. Anyway, I was smiling, and looking forward to our little outing tonight.

I was lathering my hair and got a little shampoo in my eyes. I rinsed it out, and reached out of the shower curtain to dab my eyes with a towel. When I looked up, Toni was standing still, silhouetted in the doorway, watching me from a distance.

"I'll just be a minute."

Then she stepped into the bathroom and out of the shadows, and I saw that she was naked. I was a little confused... and a little embarrassed. She crossed into a slash of golden sunlight, and it was as if she'd stepped into a spotlight on stage. She was tiny, and her skin was a creamy alabaster, spattered with soft orange freckles from head to toe. She wasn't shy about her nakedness in the least. Her tiny breasts were mostly nipple, but those were large and extended. Her body was mostly hairless, except for the light, almost transparent patch of her pubic hair that didn't hide a prominent clitoris. Her mane of red hair was striking, even clumped and sweaty. I could not help but stare at her, and not in a sexual way, not really. I could appreciate the beauty of the female form, but it was not sexually attractive to me. Toni was quite unique-looking, undraped and presented almost as a sculpture or painting. Standing starkers as she was in that shaft of sunlight, she was almost a museum installation. She wouldn't normally stand out in a crowd, this little red-haired Irish pixie, but undraped and so dramatically lit, it was hard to look away.

She crossed the tile floor toward me, and, I don't know, call me stupid, but I wasn't sure what she was doing. She came right up to the tub, gently peeled aside the shower curtain, and asked, "Okay if I join you?"

I was surprised and embarrassed and even a little disappointed, and I'm sure I blushed from head to toe.

"I… I don't think that's a good idea," I stammered like a 10-year-old.

"I won't hurt you." Her look was sweet, undemanding, not lascivious in any way. Still, I was disappointed that sex was rearing its ugly head again. It could lead to no good.

"Toni. No."

She just stood outside the tub, the shower curtain in her hand, looking into my eyes. Not staring at my naked body, not being lewd.

"I know you're lonely," she said. And that's when I started to cry.

She stepped into the tub with me, wrapped her arms around me, and kissed me, sweetly, gently, with her mouth closed. When I did not push her away, the tip of her tongue slipped between my lips for a taste.

Ω Ω Ω

Here it was again, the sweet devil of desire. I could usually fend for myself pretty well, but sometimes I just let things happen because it was easier than putting up a fight. It was too embarrassing or confusing to push someone away, someone who was merely expressing an attraction to you. I know, I know, I live in Hollywood, and I've been around the block, but this was a first for me. Of course I'd had women come on to me before, but I was good at playing dumb, oblivious, and had never had the classic college-dorm experience with another woman. It just wasn't in my playbook.

But Toni was gentle, sincere, and I discovered how empty and needy I felt. Man or woman, at that moment in my life if they'd handled me so tenderly and sweetly, it would have been hard to resist. It wasn't a *woman* who was wrapping around me in the soapy shower; it was someone who cared.

She kissed the tears from my eyes, running her fingers through the shampoo in my hair, and I allowed it, though the tears flowed even harder. She took my face in her hands, and made me look into her eyes. I tried to look away.

"Hey," she said, and I looked back at her. Her eyes were pale green, and seemed to look right inside me. Then she closed her eyes and kissed me again, and the tears stopped.

Ω Ω Ω

Somehow we ended up on my bed, and the softness of her feminine touch was startling, a little scary, but explosively erotic. I have to admit that I was the passive one, letting her do all the work, but she didn't seem to mind. On the contrary, she seemed to delight in being the explorer, the leader, the teacher. When she kissed her way down my stomach and nestled between my thighs with the light touch of her lips, then began to probe deeper with her tongue, the resulting orgasm was nearly immediate, shocking, overwhelming… and embarrassing.

I couldn't keep it from happening, but in its afterglow, I didn't think I wanted to do that again.

I broke out in gooseflesh, despite the summer heat, and shivered. When she came back up to kiss me, I could taste myself on her lips, and turned away.

Toni eased back and took my hand.

"You okay?" she asked.

I couldn't answer. I didn't know.

SEVEN

I could smell Chase's scent in the Prius. Not just the touch of vanilla and rose that seemed to symbolize her, but the sweet muskiness of her. I sat in the car in the dark garage, and just breathed her in, feeling guilty and repentant. Not that it would do her any good now.

I turned on her radio, realizing that I didn't even know what radio stations she listened to. I went through the presets, and they were predictably eclectic: New Age, Sixties, some really aggressive Hip Hop, Classical, even Metal. But it was all music, no talk. No news, no Oprah, no comedy, no words. I turned it off, and let her silence caress me.

Who was in that bed with you, Chase?

How long have you had a lover?

And what took you to that shitty little motel in Arizona?

I looked in the compartment between the seats, but all it held was some loose change, a tin of mints, a little bottle of hand sanitizer, and a microfiber cloth to wipe her sunglasses. It was all so mundane. I pushed the button over the sun visor and the garage door closed.

Settling into darkness, exhaustion and a sudden enervating *ennui* overwhelmed me. I felt smelted into place, barely able to open the door to go inside. I just stared at the steering wheel, dreading the rest of my life.

And then, I was startled by a brief vibration that made me jerk. It happened again a few moments later before the fog lifted, and I realized it was her phone ringing. I started digging around for it, and discovered it just under the driver's seat at the moment it stopped buzzing. I looked at the screen of her iPhone: I was disappointed to see that it was a text message from AT&T saying her bill was ready.

Thanks for the information.

It did, however, open my eyes to traceable evidence. My skin warmed and I felt the tips of my ears begin to burn. I swiped the screen to unlock it, and went directly to the recent calls. Right under the AT&T number was a short list of numbers from the last several days. A couple from Theresa, one to Louise's Trattoria, and five calls in a row from a Private Caller whose number I didn't recognize.

Five calls.

In a row.

All within an hour or so of one another, and all before midnight the night my wife was killed.

It took a while to realize that I had stopped breathing, that my eager heart was thumping audibly, as if trying to escape. My mouth was dry, papery. I stared blankly at the phone and the list of recent calls, then finally reached out with the tip of my finger and tapped the number.

It seemed to take forever to connect, and then, with a hesitant stutter, it began to ring. My heart beat even louder now, its pulse rushing in my ears. With a click, the ringing stopped and a voice came on the line.

A female voice. Bright and chipper.

"Hi, I'm not here, so you know what—oh, wait! I hear a car in the driveway, let me see if that's me! Nope, sorry, false alarm. Leave a message!"

Beep.

I didn't leave a message. I didn't know what to say. I just sat in the garage, and the dim overhead light extinguished itself.

The glow of the iPhone was my sole illumination, so I stared at it, and could feel my irises widen.

I tapped the Google icon, and recited the number into the phone. After moments of searching, a name and address came up to match the phone number: Antoinette McLoughlin, in Montrose, just above Glendale.

I punched the address into the GPS, pushed the garage door opener, and, despite overwhelming exhaustion, backed out into the real world again.

Ω Ω Ω

Oh, Christ; I was on the road again.

The Ventura Freeway, acting as the large intestine to the San Fernando Valley, had not yet become tumored with traffic. I actually sailed across the Valley at something close to the speed limit, until it bottlenecked a bit when it met the Hollywood Freeway. Traffic tangled again as afternoon blossomed when I passed the Santa Ana Freeway, but it was navigable, and eased up as I drove further east. My heart fluttered in my chest, fear and anticipation engaged in a grudge match. Finally, I hopped onto the Glendale Freeway, eventually finding my way to Honolulu Avenue, the anachronistically bucolic town's Main Street.

I'd been to Montrose before. It's a favorite location when you're shooting post-war small town America. The place has an old-fashioned, Middle American kind of *Leave It to Beaver* quality, though the little mom-and-pop bowling alley has since been shuttered and modernized into shops. Still, it's a diner and soda fountain kind of place, with a big jeweler's clock in the middle of the town's square, with benches and jacaranda trees, pedestrian traffic, and an old ladies' clothing shop that's been there since the 1940s. Lots of pastel.

Gaggles of young families had lately taken the place over, and I had to navigate around hot young mommies pushing their thousand-dollar strollers while their little darlings screamed and barfed on their princess dresses. I slammed on the brakes and left a screech of rubber when one such mommy, jogging in her lululemons as she pushed identical two-year-olds in her Bumbleride double stroller, ran the red light directly across my path. I burst into a cold sweat as she turned and gave me the finger. Because *she* ran the red light in front of me.

Fucking bitch.

I turned off the main drag as the GPS led me into a modest neighborhood of well-kept little homes with neat yards and relatively low rents. Toys and Hot Wheels and porch flags and SUVs and boxy little Scions were ubiquitous here, but Coventry Street itself was deserted. The GPS, speaking in the voice of John Cleese, directed me to the last house on the left. I parked across the street, and took its temperature.

The house at 1795-97 Coventry was a tiny, single-story Craftsman, built of dark wood and rounded grey stones, and had been converted into a duplex some years ago. The porch overhang shaded two entrances, with a stone and masonry wall dividing them. There was a dusty Mini Cooper parked in the driveway, with a vanity plate that read RT ONE. *Right one? Arty one?* I'm guessing the latter. It looked like it hadn't been through a car wash in over a year, that's how arty it was; some comedic firebrand had finger-painted *eat me* in the dirt on the back window. There was a rock garden outside, and a couple of environmentally conscious cacti. A litter of pinwheels sat motionless in the summer stillness around a barrel cactus. An antique wheelbarrow was piled with dirt, out of which a ventriloquist's dummy was poking his head. A Wheel of Fortune, faded from years in the sun, provided a backdrop to the mesquite tree, from which dolls were hanging by the neck from thin, colorful ribbons. Yeah, *arty one* for sure.

I got out of the car, crossed the street, and climbed onto the front porch. Antoinette's address was the unit on the right, so I rang the bell, which chimed like a call to Sunday services, deep and resonant. It died out into silence as I waited. A small dog started barking from the adjoining unit, its voice angry and high-pitched. It scratched madly against the door, and I did my best to ignore it. I rang again, just as a gust of Santa Ana wind, hot and forceful, huffed across the yard, setting the pinwheels into rattly motion. The Wheel of Fortune creaked and grunted as it made a half turn. Still no answer, just the little mutt next door getting more and more pissed at me. I tried to peer through the pebbled glass window at the top of the door, but couldn't make out a thing. Old mahogany blinds in the front window were clenched tight.

I knocked, knowing it wouldn't do any good, and called out to her.

"Antoinette!"

Another gust of wind was the only response, shoving sheets of newspaper down the still deserted street.

I went over and knocked on the door to the adjoining unit, and the nasty little mongrel squeaked and ran whimpering to the back of the house. It was easy to call the little fucker's bluff. But no one answered there, either.

I wasn't prepared to give up. I didn't come all the way out to Mayberry just to knock and accept no response. I looked at Antoinette's dense maple door. It wanted me to open it. I looked down the street, which remained empty. I looked at the doorknob, crusted as it was with decades of dark grey hand grime. It was begging for me to use it. There had to be a reason that, when I reached out and gripped it, it turned so easily in my hand. It wasn't even locked. The ancient hardware clicked and clacked, and the heavy door sighed open with nary a creak.

With the lights out and the blinds drawn, the little domicile was surprisingly cool; they really knew how to build a house in the days before air conditioning. It was dark, too, though buttery afternoon light leaked through from the back of the little bungalow, reflecting off the high gloss of the polished bare oak floor. I stepped into the gloom of the tiny living room. A row of antique dolls in lacy dresses sat atop the stone mantel over the rock fireplace. The bust of a Devil sat on the grate in the fireplace, grinning a plastic smile. All of the furnishings were faded and elderly—I'm sorry, *vintage*—and the eclectic lack of style pronounced itself stylishly. There were two racks of clothing in the middle of the room, as well as a row of three dressmaker's dummies, each attired in 1940s couture. There was a stack of costume sketches on top of the low, wide, coffee table that sat on faux elephant's feet. At least, I hope they were faux. An old neon bowling alley clock was on the wall above the fireplace; the second hand labored around its face with a grinding sound, but the time was off by hours. A parrot stared at me from an ornate iron cage. I wondered why it was so silent until I saw sand leaking from its rear end. Bad taxidermy.

I stepped back toward the hallway, and the worn crocheted rug slipped out from under my foot; I had to grab for the wall to keep from hitting the floor. The little dog next door started barking again. I kicked the wall, and heard him run away, yelping as if I'd kicked him in the nuts.

Next came the little kitchen. Its window was uncovered, wide open, and sunlight was eager to make its way inside. The walls were yellow, the appliances varying vintage pastels: green refrigerator, pink stove, pale blue sink, all self-consciously eclectic, but it seemed to work anyway. Dried flower bouquets were set on the table and windowsill, and abundant fruits and vegetables grew fragrant in the sun. I'll bet they were organic. But the kitchen, charming as it was, provided none of the answers I sought, so I dismissed it.

The little home was only one room deeper, so I stepped back into the narrow hallway to enter it. The smell was my first warning.

Okay, you know what's coming, and if I'd been reading this or watching it on TV, so would I. But it was different living it. I guess in real life we're a little bit dumber than in the movies, or at least we don't quite hew to the three-act formula so slavishly. I did not expect Antoinette McLoughlin's captivating little bedroom to be an abattoir.

I'd experienced the post-cleanup scene at Sheffler's in Salome, but here was the slaughter in all its three-strip Technicolor glory. A tiny, naked redhead lay sprawled across her bed, skin like porcelain and every inch of it dressed in freckles. But the body had been rent asunder, torn open, its innards outward, sliced open from groin to chest. Blood had shot against the walls, soaking the framed photos on the headboard with a darkening glisten. The woman's smile had been enlarged, the edges of her mouth cut from one ear to the other. A knife or something had slashed viciously across the chest, cutting a line across her meager, girlish breasts. Her nakedness was as horrid as the violence done to it, and I had to look away, suddenly dizzy, choking on the heat, returning to the magic land of *déjà vu*. The brutality I'd so laughingly, even mockingly depicted on *Slaughter* was not nearly so amusing in real life. The body was no temple, my oeuvre proclaimed, it was merely meat. At a remove from the prop-shop body parts, that may have been so.

But having seen my wife revealed to me in a blanket of her own blood, and now, confronted with a human being splayed mercilessly before me in loving close-up, a once-living-now-dead lovely young woman lying in her own offal without further commercial interruption… I was not amused. I was not entertained. I hated the flesh and blood that comprised me. I wished I were without body: mere thought, mere memory.

Alas, I was not.

No. I was in the Small Town American hamlet of Montrose, mind and body reeling, standing in the middle of the blood-spattered bedroom of a petite, once lovely stranger, a *redheaded* stranger, struggling not to look at her mangled corpse, in a time machine tumbler that took me to a little motel in a little desert town in Arizona, smelling the rotting-copper stench of decaying blood and flesh, confirming my lifelong suspicion that Life is not Beautiful, after all.

Somehow, I had become the sun at the center of a solar system of death.

I was melting.

My skin was suddenly drenched in a foul wash of perspiration, and I leaned weakly against the wall. I could feel the blood rush from my face, my legs wobbling, struggling to breathe but choking on the taste of blood in the air.

No more death, I begged the Fates. Would that it were so.

And then, a vibration in my pocket brought me back to earth. It repeated itself, begging for attention. I reached in and pulled out my nagging phone. It was Sheriff Hardy calling. I stared at his name and number as it buzzed in my quaking, sweaty hand. I looked up at the corpse in the bed opposite me, the body of the young woman staring, unblinking, through wide, green, accusatory eyes, deep into my soul. The phone hummed again, allowing me to look away from the slaughtered lamb… but there was no way I was going to answer it. I was drenched in guilt just standing intimately in the bedroom with this naked, mutilated creature. The phone went still, and I left the little house.

Ω Ω Ω

I sat in nauseous confusion in Chase's Prius across from the duplex for long, lonely minutes, wondering what to do. The silence was suddenly broken when a half-dozen pubescent boys rounded the corner and whizzed by on their skateboards, shouting and declaiming one another, flipping their boards, tumbling to the street, and climbing back on to continue their play. A couple of them threw looks at me, the stranger sitting alone on their street, but they had no time for me; they had shins and elbows to scrape and scar. The street went quiet again, and I was the only one who knew what lay behind door number two.

I couldn't put this off any longer. I returned Hardy's call.

"Mr. Turrentine, good to hear from you. I just tried to reach you."

"Yes, I know," I phumphered; "I'm returning your call."

"Just wanted to keep in touch, sir," he told me. "Not much new to report, I'm afraid. Only the fact that there was no evidence of sexual assault. I hope that puts your mind at ease at least a little bit."

I closed my eyes. No, my mind was not eased, not even a little bit.

"Sheriff…" I choked.

"Yes?"

"I have something to report to *you*…"

Ω Ω Ω

The little neighborhood was no longer quiet. Three LAPD patrol cars, an ambulance, god knows how many unmarked official vehicles, and a rodeo of news trucks jammed Coventry Street. Bland, whitewashed blue-eyed blonde news reporters of disposable and forgettable beauty, daydreaming of movie-star careers, did their stand-ups within inches of one another, delighted that the story had broken just in time for their dinnertime broadcasts. The live remotes fit perfectly around the commercial breaks; too bad it wasn't in the middle of May sweeps. August would have to do.

I sat in the living room of Antoinette McLoughlin's little house, peering through the wooden slats. It was a hungry crowd out there beyond the police tape. I sat on a leather couch opposite a rather enormous local homicide detective who spilled over the edges of what appeared to be an Eames chair. Detective Maldonado was well over six feet tall, with a beetled brow that hooded deep-set brown eyes. His hair was thick and so black that it was almost blue, making me think, for some reason, of Superman. His build, however, was far less heroic. He was gargantuan, and stuffed into an ill-fitting Hugo Boss suit that he probably bought second hand. A roll of fat extruded over his shirt collar, which, despite the oppressive heat, was buttoned tight and knotted with a red tie. His shoes had thick soles, but were well worn at the heels. His hands were meaty; his wedding ring was being swallowed by the flesh that surrounded it. His nails were immaculately manicured.

I'd told him everything about finding the phone number on Chase's phone and tracing it here, to this hipster bungalow in a decidedly non-hipster neighborhood. I'd told him everything about the discovery of the body. But I did not tell him about the little red hair I had found in Chase's bed.

He just stared at me from under that Neanderthal brow, not breaking the silence, waiting for me to divulge something more. My guilt, perhaps. But I had nothing left to say. He tried to wait me out, but I was done. I wanted to go home.

We both turned to watch the EMTs roll the gurney with the covered body down the hallway and out the front door. I peered through the blinds as they emerged into the sunlight, as the press swarmed like lawyers in an emergency room around them.

Maldonado returned his patient gaze to me.

Finally, giving in, he broke his own silence.

"So," he sighed. "You didn't know Ms. McLoughlin."

"Never met her."

"Did you know *of* her?"

"I never heard Chase mention her, if that's what you mean."

"But she was a friend of your wife's?"

"Not that I know of. But that doesn't mean she wasn't."

"You don't know your wife's friends?"

"My wife didn't have many friends. But we work in a business with lots of acquaintances. It wouldn't surprise me that she knew her. But it would surprise me if they were close."

Well, that wasn't exactly true. I had a little red hair in a Kleenex in my pocket that hinted at extreme intimacy, but that was my secret. My mind was roiling. Had this girl been in bed with my wife? Had she been having an affair with her? I'd never seen the slightest interest or inclination toward women from Chase, most certainly not when I'd hinted at the possibility; it just didn't seem to make any sense.

But here I sat under the inscrutable, watchful, disturbingly unblinking gaze of LAPD Homicide Detective Raul Maldonado. This guy must have been a crackerjack poker player. I was drenched in sweat, but he, despite the black suit, the tight collar and tie, and his considerable girth, was fruit salad cool.

"Did your wife have enemies?"

Only me, is what I should have said, but I didn't.

"Everybody liked Chase. She was kind and generous, if a bit shy. Again, she really sort of kept to herself."

"And you don't know Ms. McLoughlin."

"No."

"Never met her."

"Not to my recollection."

"But it's possible that you've met her at some time in the past."

"Possible, but not likely."

"Not likely? Why is that?"

"I would probably remember."

"Why is that? Do you find her attractive?"

"I would remember because she was petite, red-haired, unique-looking."

He nodded, not taking his eyes off of me. And not blinking, either; the Bizarro-world version of Hannibal Lecter or something. His stare felt like the glare of a 10K on me.

I tried to wait him out, but he had more patience than me.

"Do you think," I asked, "that she was killed by the same person who murdered my wife?"

He blinked, but never released me from his gaze.

"I'd be astonished if she weren't," he answered coolly. His look indicted me, threatened me, but he just sat there, a malevolent Santa in an Eames chair, waiting for me to tell him what I wanted for Christmas.

"The husband of the victim is always the first suspect, isn't he," I said.

He nodded. "Yep. And he's usually guilty."

"And you think I murdered my wife. And this woman."

"The thought hadn't crossed my mind, frankly. Why, should I?"

"Of course not!"

He let a trace of a smile sneak onto his face.

"You don't seem like the type."

It sounded like an insult.

"*Did* you kill your wife?"

"No."

He stood up and slapped imaginary dust from his palms on his thighs.

"Good enough for me," he said. "I think we've got everything we need here, Mr. Turrentine. You're free to go."

"Really?"

"Unless there's something else you'd like to tell me."

I just shook my head and he lifted his hand, guiding me to the hall.

I never stopped, never looked back as I stormed the gauntlet of the media; as they swarmed around me, I just flipped an elegant middle finger, slid into Chase's car, and pulled through them, not giving a shit whether I hit one of them or not.

Ω Ω Ω

By now, the drive back to Woodland Hills was back to its normal afternoon clot. I sat behind an immense truck with Baja California plates, idling and spewing thick black smoke from its rusted emission pipes. Deadlocked in a sea of single-passenger vehicles, I was shrouded in insignificance. I was the Invisible Man, too unworthy to even garner suspicion in the death of my wife. In my profession, I toiled in obscurity until that plug had been pulled. I lived on my wife's savings and tiny residual checks for work I had done years ago, each of them losing weight as the time since their original broadcast had passed.

There's not a soul on the planet that would give a shit if some alien transport hovered overhead and sucked me aboard to whisk me away to the planet Oblivion. If my heart stopped and left me dead behind the wheel, it would only piss people off because I was blocking traffic. Someone would no doubt have to pay the Times for my obituary to be listed; I wonder if my agent would bother. Not that I deserved better. I was the master of my domain, but that domain didn't extend beyond my little office at the back of the house. My world had shrunk, my hairline receded, my waistline expanded. And here I was, in the wake of Chase's horrific death, feeling sorry for myself.

What an asshole.

Redemption, remember? I had a cause, an excuse to take up space on the planet. I had loved Chase more than I had loved anyone else, and it was getting easier to bring those memories back. It was the hate that had faded, if not been erased. If I had any purpose whatsoever, it was to avenge her, to touch once again the spirit I had so mercilessly abused and ignored.

Whereas I was at first resigned to being stuck here at the nexus of the Hollywood and Ventura Freeways, now I was getting pissed. Get me the fuck out of here! Not that it helped, of course; the traffic was at a standstill for another fifteen minutes before it started to budge. It was another forty-five minutes before I reached the Topanga turnoff, and another twenty before I reached the house.

I pulled into the garage, turned on the sprinklers, and entered the kitchen through the garage door.

I went directly to Chase's bedroom, which had once been *our* bedroom. She'd always insisted on sleeping on the left side, closest to the bathroom. It didn't matter to me. We'd played in that bed, she'd cried in that bed, I'd held her in that bed and actually made her feel better. It might have been a long time ago and a galaxy far, far away, but this bed maintained its secrets, held the joy and its decay deep inside. I saw us from the mirrored closets, tussling and laughing, naked and rapturous. I saw myself banned from the room in a storm of recrimination. But mostly, I saw silence, a closed box of Chase Willoughby, dying like the unattended marigolds on the windowsill.

What have I missed? What didn't I see? What had I closed my eyes to? What did I make her turn to?

I couldn't take her bedroom anymore, and went downstairs and into her studio.

The paintings, all in rage and pain, glared at me, pissed at me. I knew the Primal Scream series, and felt responsible that her art had taken such a dark turn during our marriage. But there was memorabilia of the life that had passed before on those walls, as well. Framed photos of her and her parents. The *TV Guide* cover from *The Crazy Frazees*. A cast and crew photo, with the face of the slimeball producer who impregnated her and tossed her career over a cliff blacked out in felt marker. Some guest star photos from failed pilots: one with a very young George Clooney, another with a very old Tony Curtis. And finally, the last stop on the wall of fame, a framed color shot of the cast and crew on the last day of shooting *Frankel's People*.

Chase looked luminous at the center of the frame, hugging Dermot Mulroney and Eddie Izzard. Her smile could not have been more open and sincere, expressing a joy I'd successfully extinguished over the years. I scanned the happy faces; this was obviously a warm set. I'd seen them before. *Slaughter* was definitely not one of those.

Then, I saw it, peeking out at me: an elfin little redhead, perhaps the happiest of the bunch, at the center of a cluster who lifted her head high so she could be as tall as the rest of them, looking different not covered in blood, her smile narrower than the murderer's blade had left it.

Antoinette McLoughlin.

So there was a link. But I didn't know what to make of it.

Chase Willoughby and Antoinette McLoughlin occupied the same frame.

ΣIGHT

Hollywood Forever has to be the most embarrassing name for a cemetery in the history of buried bodies. Located smack in the center of the fading, industrial, primarily Latino east end of Hollywood, right over the backyard fence of Paramount Studios, it was the resting ground for luminaries from Rudolph Valentino to Peter Lorre to Jane Mansfield to Tyrone Power to a couple of the Ramones. Buses filled with Japanese tourists made daily pilgrimages there, and during the summer they'd host outside screenings of horror movies against the crypt walls.

Classy joint.

I could not believe the size of the crowd that overflowed the charming little Old World chapel that morning for Chase's memorial. The anticipated news trucks and their collective spires of antennae huddled in the circular drive just inside the graveyard's gates, and veins of asphalt that meandered throughout the park-like grounds were filled with cars. I'd gotten there early, not wanting to be photographed arriving, but the media had staked their stalking grounds long before I ever arrived.

There was no family there, at least not of a biological nature; but the rainbow coalition of the actors who made up *The Crazy Frazees* were all in attendance. The female former moppets from the show, none of whom had been employed since then, were startlingly grown-up. Each of them was troweled with makeup so thick that it left their features immobilized, despite their tender years, with yeasty, expanded lips that were covered in wet, red lip gloss. The youngest, Darlene Harvey, who was only six years old at the time of the show, had already been inflated with pneumatic breast implants that must have given her back muscles an extreme workout. Each of them was making the most of the exposure they'd get on the evening news. The boys were there, too, sullen-faced with a week's growth of beard. One of them wore a black hoodie out of respect. The other three had ties on over their colorful shirts, with jeans that hung low to reveal gym-sculpted abs and a waxed pubis. Peter Garrity, the evil producer with the potent spermatozoa, tried to slink in unnoticed under dark glasses and a slicked-back mane of now-stark-white hair, but Channel 7 recognized him, and ran close to track him into the chapel.

Jerry Atherton, dressed in Armani and shod with ridiculous Italian shoes with incredibly long-barreled toes that looked like they belonged in Oz, was there with his twenty-year-old date, who looked sixteen, despite her tasteful Cavalli dress, which was at least *mostly* black. Theresa Black, squat and resplendent in sturdy boots and belted black chamois that had to be worth more than the ten percent she was giving up with Chase's demise, was surrounded by a coterie of fellow agents from SAA, all male, and all in matching black European suits, identifiable only by their ties, which were a mix of red, blue, and green.

Among the throng of fans in their thirties and forties was an assortment of washed-up middle-aged and older stars of long-gone, unremembered series. Each of them had flared brightly in a single vehicle, then left at the off-ramp of their series' cancellation, never to be heard from again. But here they were as if it were an autograph weekend at the Beverly Garland Holiday Inn in Universal City, faces surgically tightened into ever-present, impossibly white smiles, brows incapable of human expression, their hair frosted and dyed into colors not found in nature. And this was the same for the men *and* the women. There were no A-listers in attendance.

I recognized one group from the Bravo network; I guess they had not yet given up hope for the series. Maldonado was there, too, in the same black suit he'd worn at the little house in Montrose. I almost didn't recognize Hardy, as I'd only seen him in uniform. He nodded to me respectfully, clearly uncomfortable in jacket and tie.

Most obtrusive, of course, was the army of doughy, greasy-haired, perspiring paparazzi: these cave-dwelling parasites with giant telephoto lenses searched the crowd mercilessly for tears, facelifts, and embarrassing expressions. These bottom-feeding salamanders of the press breathed foul air heavily through their open mouths as they tried in vain to get crotch shots of the female celebrities as they exited their limos or took their seats.

I was the only one sitting in the section reserved for family, the only occupant in a section comprised of two rows of a half-dozen chairs each. It felt right to be alone.

The overtaxed air conditioning had failed as the chapel filled with silent observers, in the thick of one of LA's hottest summers. Fans on high stands were quickly whipped into position, but all they did was move the stuffy, overly perfumed air around. The onlookers fanned their gleaming faces with their memorial programs, and organ music began as everyone took their seats.

At the head of the Chapel lay the closed casket with Chase's corrupted body preserved within. Ornate sprays of flora filled the open space with bright colors that seemed to be an insult to the solemnity of the proceedings. I could only stare at the burnished black oak coffin and imagine what was within, how she'd been stitched and spackled together in a drastic attempt to restore some semblance of her unique beauty. That the coffin was closed made my dark imagination run free, and the nausea that had been eating holes in my stomach lining since that first call from Sheriff Hardy was getting noisy.

Religion had played no part in our lives, and certainly had provided no salvation to Chase. Still, this testament to her life demanded someone to minister to the world her valedictory, and the roughly handsome, Nordic-looking six-foot Methodist seemed cast by Lynn Kressel. His voice was mellifluous and calm, respectful and gentle. He spoke as if he knew her, but it was clear that they'd never met. I could not pay attention to the tired bloviations his job required; I could only stare at the coffin and feel my throat constrict. I caught the occasional phrase—"Chase wouldn't want to see the tears spilling from her friends' eyes"—but it was just so much verbiage. I'd been there for Chase's tears, as well as her laughter, and I'd seen both end in a vat of resignation.

It took me a while to realize silence had fallen. I looked up from Chase's casket to see the good Reverend looking to me with a beatific smile, his hand outstretched in welcome. It took a moment for the webs to clear and realize that I was the first one who was supposed to speak my memories of my late, beloved spouse. Whispers and shuffled feet filled the silent gap as I came to my senses. I had notes I'd made on a couple of folded sheets of damp blue paper that I was worrying with my moist, shaking hands; when I stood, my legs buckled in nervousness as I made my way to the front of the chapel. The minister moved aside as I lay my pages down to sleep on the lectern, my hands shaking uncontrollably. At least I could hide them here.

I looked up, and a sea of wide-eyed, eager faces were focused on me, hundreds of them, waiting to hear what I had to say about this beautiful woman who meant something to them. I was their fantasy; I slept with this goddess every night, we had conjugated, shared an intimacy that they had no hope of ever experiencing. I was their surrogate, their direct link to life with the glamorous Chase Willoughby.

I couldn't look at them; their faces were too hungry, too eager, too prying. Some of them had tears in their eyes, sniffling and wiping away their sorrow with Kleenex. I looked down at the crumpled pages I'd printed out, and the words lost focus. I just couldn't read them.

I looked up again and opened my mouth. But at the sight of the sadness that was being fanned through the whitewashed chapel with the raw, exposed, dark wood beams, I felt my mouth pulled back, my throat shutting down. I clenched my eyes shut to stave off the rush of sudden, unexpected tears. No words would come. I could not speak. Trying to control my breathing, I returned to my seat, broken.

The crowd was embarrassed, maybe for me, maybe for making a shambles of the event. It was too much for me to take.

NINE

It was done. I didn't regret it, I guess, so much as I just wanted to put the sex behind me. It couldn't be undone, but I could move on, and I was ready to do so.

"You still want to go dancing tonight, don't you?"

"I don't know, Toni. I think I just want to stay home."

"Unacceptable answer. You've just-stayed-home for far too long." She sat up, covering herself with the sheet. She could tell I was discomfited, maybe filled with regret, and tried to push it aside and return me to a happier place.

"I will accept no change in plan. We're getting dressed up for a night on the town. I'll take charge of wardrobe, and we will dance and party until the clubs close down."

It sounded like work to me.

"No," I sighed. "I was never a party girl, and I don't think I want to start now."

"Fine. Then we go dancing, put all the bullshit behind us, and have a good time until you're ready to go back to your lonely little Duxiana bed. Okay? Okay." And with that, she leapt out of bed, unembarrassed by her nakedness, and strode on tiptoe across the parquet floor.

I huddled under the blankets, shy and embarrassed, as Toni went through my closet. She was much tinier than me, but I was guessing that she could find something that would fit. Once she disappeared into the walk-in closet, I emerged from the bedclothes, strode quickly across to the antique Irish wardrobe, and quickly climbed into my underwear, feeling un-wholesomely exposed. I threw my silk Chinese robe on over my green La Perla dainties, feeling foolish and girly as Toni emerged in a tight little red jersey dress that clung tight to her skin. She rolled up the hem, which was the only place it was too long for her, and when she shook out her copper hair, all traces of tomboy evaporated.

"What do you think?" she asked.

"It looks great on you!" I told her, truthfully.

"Should I wear a bra?" Her nipples were proudly evident.

"Only if you don't want everyone staring at your tits."

"Maybe I do!" And she started laughing. Her face blossomed into a joyous, simple elation so sunny that it was hard not to be infected by it. I laughed, too, and the awkwardness of what had just transpired began to fall away. I think she was being careful not to acknowledge it.

"Now," she said. "What are we going to do with you?"

She started going through the dresses, pulling out the slinkiest, most revealing ones she could find. She held up a loose, clingy Versace I'd worn to the Heal the Bay benefit last summer at the Santa Monica pier.

"This is the one for you tonight!" she proclaimed.

"Too sexy!"

"There's no such thing!" She giggled again. "Just let me be your costume designer for the night, okay? You've got the perfect body for dresses like this. So don't deny the world the experience."

I felt silly, I felt self-conscious, but I also felt ready to emerge from my cocoon, at least for the evening. She extended the dress toward me, urging me to take it and put it on. My smile dam broke, and I laughed at her insistence. It made us both feel good.

"Okay, *fine*! You win!"

"No, *you* win."

I stepped into the pale green raw silk dress, which crackled with static electricity against my skin. I felt caressed by it, it fell into place so perfectly. It had been a while since I felt so much like a girl.

"Lose the bra," Toni said.

"No!" I objected.

"Look, with a body like yours under a dress like that, it's like artillery or something, like you're wearing a chastity belt. You were born sexy, so *be* sexy."

Sexy: everything good and everything bad in my life came from that cursed blessing.

"I like the bra," I said. "It's La Perla."

"Well, for God's sake, at least let it show." She reached over and adjusted the neckline so that the silky brassiere could be seen cradling my breasts. "You know, I think that's even better. Good choice."

We stood and regarded ourselves in the full-length mirror.

"You know, we're a couple of pretty hot chicks, aren't we?" It was as if our little conjunction had never happened, that we had never been intimate in my bed, even though it had just transpired. Toni was more perceptive than I'd given her credit for. And she made me laugh again.

And, as a matter of fact, we *were* a couple of pretty hot chicks.

"You want me to do your makeup?" she asked.

Ω Ω Ω

We were starving, so we got a quick bite at Kate Mantilini's on Ventura. It was early for the dinner crowd, so we got a seat right away. Warren Beatty was with Annette Bening and their kids in a corner booth away from the *hoi polloi*. Kim Basinger was alone at a table not far away, picking at a salad, the paparazzi having already forgotten her. I hoped I would age as well as she.

We went unrecognized, which was a relief, seated right in the middle of the restaurant. It was dark now, and I was ravenous. I hadn't had bread in ages, and when they brought a basket of rolls still steaming from the oven, I tore one apart and submerged it in olive oil and gobbled it down as if it were the last supper. I looked up and Toni was smiling at me.

"What?"

"It's nice to see you enjoy your food. I'll bet you've been eating like a girl for a long time. Looks like you've lost a little weight."

"I can't remember having been this hungry. I think I'll even eat some *meat*!"

"Oh, you naughty little carnivore!"

The waiter took our order and nodded approvingly when I ordered a rare steak and sweet potato fries. "I like a girl who eats like a man!" he said. He was thin, even a bit wispy, and his manner exaggeratedly effeminate. He obviously had worn big plugs in his ears when they were fashionable, as the holes remained, making his lobes long and limp.

"I'll bet he prefers a man who eats like a man," Toni whispered to me once his back was turned. We both broke out into peals of mean-girl laughter, and he turned back to us with a giant smile on his face.

"Tell me! I want a laugh, too!"

That made us laugh all over again.

"Oh, no," Toni told him, "it's at your expense!"

"You are so *bad*," he said. Then he leaned down to my ear and whispered confidentially, "You know, I still have a poster of Ellie Frazee on my bedroom wall!" then rushed our order back to the kitchen.

"Somebody's got a fan," Toni said. "Maybe we'll get a free dessert!"

We did.

Ω Ω Ω

Unbelievably, I'd devoured most of the slab of cow that had overhung my oversized plate, as well as the preceding salad and the gratis crème brûlée after. I was having a protein rush, a surge of superpowers hitherto unknown. I'd lived on garden clippings and bean curd for so long that I forgot what it was like to dine like a flyover American. I wouldn't want to do it often, but rather than making me logy, if anything, it made me a little hyper, eager to be out, even looking forward to some loud music and a good time.

"Where would you like to go?" Toni asked.

"Just someplace that nobody knows me." I just wanted to be one of the crowd, not a tabloid princess whose claim to fame was a shitty sitcom and a fucked-up pregnancy.

"Well, that isn't LA," Toni said. "Your fame and infamy is a beacon here. But I've got an idea."

"Tell me."

"Let's go to the desert!"

"Jesus, Toni, it's ninety-seven degrees in Woodland Hills and you want to go to the desert?"

"Absolutely! It's early; we've got the time and the air conditioning. Let's get out of Dodge!"

It was nice not to be making the decisions for a change. Jimmy had become so passive that he would never take command. Anything was okay with him. I was sick of having to be the responsible one, the one who gave a shit about anything, and it was nice to let Toni take control.

"You're the driver," I said, and she whipped out of the parking lot in a rubber-burning U-turn, and flew onto the freeway and headed east.

Ω Ω Ω

Once we got past the San Gabriel Valley and the blinding lights of Los Angeles County, the deepening sky presented itself in awesome focus. Constellations shimmered against a black velvet background, surrounded by the spilled jewelry of the heavens' royalty. It was kind of magnificent, really, this view that was hidden from city dwellers. The air was hot, dry, and unscented here in the less-developed expanse of Southern California, and I opened my window, letting the hot wind whip my hair into a tangled mess. The Sixties music that she'd loaded onto her iPod was the perfect soundtrack for a night like this as we zipped from lane to lane at 80 miles per hour in her nimble little Mini Cooper.

By the time we pulled off onto Highway 111, melting into Palm Canyon Drive, the main drag was bustling with tan, leathery, lizard-skinned locals, middle-aged gay bears trotting from Starbucks to TCBY in flip-flops and beige cargo shorts, European tourist families with weird sunglasses and bright pink fanny packs, and students looking to raise a little hell. We zipped around the corner and into an uncrowded public parking lot. I gasped when we stepped out of the car and into the Palm Springs broiler. It must have been at least 110 degrees.

A dry heat, yeah, but Jesus! Toni linked my arm in hers, and we walked in jolly step, like Dorothy and the Cowardly Lion, around the corner onto North Palm Canyon.

Las Casuelas seemed to be the town's heartbeat, serving up giant margaritas with chips and salsa to already-toasted, red, sweaty-faced imbibers on the patio, as a greying band of classic rockers pounded out "My Sharona" in a perfect, soulless replication of the Knack record. The smoking crowd on the sidewalk luxuriated under the misters that sprayed overhead, the mist evaporating in the night's blast furnace before it hit the ground. This wasn't my idea of a night on the town.

"Um… this isn't exactly what I had in mind, Toni."

She laughed. God, she was always laughing.

"Just stick with me, kid!" and she kept hold of my arm in a kind of high-school-best-girlfriend kind of way. "We're just starting."

She dragged me into a place called Zeldaz on the corner just past the Mexican place. House music blared, and the pounding bass made the floor-to-ceiling windows vibrate to the beat, trying to disguise the fact that it was really too early for any kind of crowd. There might have been a dozen people inside at most, and the massive room suddenly was really depressing. Each of them looked at us hungrily, as if they were hunters seeking edible prey. No one was on the dancefloor, despite the desperately ear-shattering electronics. Ten of the dozen patrons were men, blow-dried and hairy-chested, and their capped teeth and dyed hair made them look older, rather than providing the hoped-for disguise of youth and fitness. They literally roamed the boards, drinks in hand, when we walked in, as if staking their claims. Two women sat at the bar, dressed like twins, though one of them was Asian and the other some kind of self-styled princess. They both had long nails, tube tops over surgically enhanced bustlines, and healthy muffin tops sprouting over their low, wispy skirts. For some reason, the barracudas writhing across the dancefloor toward us had kept their distance from the competition at the bar. Perhaps they'd been rebuffed.

We blew our kisses and were out the door within two minutes, the militant bass beat still throbbing in my medulla oblongata. We headed south and grabbed a couple of iced lattes at the Coffee Bean & Tea Leaf across the street. Most of the desert action had moved to Indian Wells and Rancho Mirage, but that's not the kind of night either of us was looking for. Just some music and fun and dancing where maybe *we* were the only ones dressed to impress.

The next stop was a place called Gumbo Joe's, and there was already a crowd forming outside. We downed the dregs of our lattes and went inside. The playlist had at least gotten as far as the Black Eyed Peas, which was an improvement. And though I wasn't exactly seeking a *fashionista* haunt, we could have done better than the T-shirts and cargo shorts this crowd had chosen as their uniform. It was fine for our first way station on this night of freedom, but I wasn't ready for drinks yet, and the dancefloor was still abandoned. I certainly was not going to be the girl to christen it. We were way overdressed for Gumbo Joe and his family.

"Strike two," Toni called out over the music. "Let's blow this hot dog stand."

And we did.

Alternate Route was just down the block over a Ben & Jerry's, so I didn't have high hopes about its entertainment value, but once we went in, we found a place that was already in swing, kind of cozy, youngish enough, with music that wasn't something you'd find on the radio forty times a day. The dancefloor was on the small side, but couples were bopping and grinding and generally enjoying themselves already. It seemed a welcoming and friendly place, and we felt comfortable. There seemed a pretty even mix of men and women, and a low percentage of amphibious trawlers.

Toni turned to me for my approval, and I nodded.

"What do you want to drink?" she asked me.

"A merlot. But let me get it."

"Not a chance in hell. Be right back."

I knew I drew looks when I crossed the room; it happens all the time, it's a fact of life. Not bragging; it's given me more grief than pleasure. I've learned to just ignore it and not make eye contact. But I was very aware of how Toni had dressed me, and how exaggerated my femininity might have been. I was high enough on estrogen, but I know the effect was enhanced on this night. I hoped my pheromones were keeping to themselves, but I knew I threw off a womanly scent I could not control.

I found a tiny empty table in a corner, and took a seat, making sure Toni saw where I was going. She waited in a cluster at the bar for our drinks, and the room throbbed to the Arctic Monkeys. I could feel eyes on me, could practically feel their caress, and it made me want to back away. Maybe this wasn't such a good idea, after all. Maybe I should be back in Woodland Hills working on my art. Yeah, maybe I should be hiding in my studio so that I don't run into my husband and hear him blasting brutal Japanese horror movies in the home theater instead of writing, hoping that we don't meet in the kitchen and start yelling at one another. Maybe I should be in that little house, dreaming of escape, huddled in a blanket of self-loathing, hiding from the world outside so they don't see how much I've fucked up a promising life. Maybe I didn't want to smile anymore, or have any friends, or dream any dreams that didn't wake me up screaming or in tears.

Considering the alternative, collecting stares from strangers in a bar in Palm Springs wasn't so bad.

I looked back at Toni, who had worked her way halfway through the line. And then, that sinking feeling as my eyes locked with a guy who was staring at me, waiting for me to return his gaze. I knew he considered himself handsome, and though he was probably about my age, he was far from my type. He had the torso and the hair, but he was just too fucking confident for me, like he could have me if he wanted me. Well, think again, Mister. He wasn't bad-looking, in fact, I'll bet most women would have been attracted to him, but he was just too aware of his appearance—maybe a bit too metrosexual—for my tastes. Any man who puts that much time and energy into his look kind of turns me off.

I looked away as quickly as I could, but it was too late. I'd been caught in his bright blue high beams, and he started to cross the room toward me. I started shuffling through my purse, just to have somewhere else to look. That wouldn't last long. He pulled up the chair opposite mine and grinned a bright, white, but slightly snaggled smile. I kind of liked that his teeth weren't perfect.

"Mind if I join you?"

"I'm waiting for my friend over there. She's getting our drinks."

"She?"

Oh, shit. I might as well as handed him an engraved invitation.

"My friend."

"I'll keep you company until she gets here. Looks like the bartender is kind of overwhelmed." He looked at me with unsubtle desire. "And so am I, to tell you the truth."

Ugh. I hate lines. Why not just say hi and ask me my sign, for God's sake.

He held out his hand to me as he swept into the seat right next to me. "I'm Jaxon," he said. "With an X."

I needed a publicist to protect me from social intercourse. But here I was, alone against Jaxon with an X. I wished Toni would hurry the fuck up. I was being forced into introducing myself; I could see no way around it. But I kept my hand to myself.

"Chase."

"I know."

Oh, shit. Outed again.

"You know?"

"Oh, yeah. I used to pleasure myself to your picture on my *Crazy Frazees* lunchbox when I was thirteen."

Sudden nausea coursed through me as I stood and pulled away from him. "Okay, that's it. Not nice to meet you, Jaxon with an X. Go fuck yourself."

"Hey," he said, mystified by my angry response, "I meant it as a compliment." I flipped him off and headed to the bar. Toni was just placing her order when I grabbed her by the shoulder and turned her to me.

"I was just ordering!"

"Not here."

"Somebody bother you?"

"You could say that."

So we left the air-conditioned comfort of Alternate Route and headed back into the blast furnace of Palm Canyon Drive.

I could escape Jaxon with an X, but I couldn't escape Ellie Frazee, that bitch.

"I've got an idea," Toni said, her face lighting up. She hailed a cab and we hopped in. "Take us to the Riviera," she told the cabbie, who whisked us away. We were there in a couple of minutes; it couldn't have been a mile away. Feeling guilty, I over-tipped him.

So we pulled up into a 1950s retro, oversized Googie-style hotel, luxuriating in its vintage trendiness, huge murals of Rat Packers and Rat Pack Fuckers on the walls. Frank was singing "Come Fly with Me" over the speakers throughout the compound, and the lobby was filled with California casual young adults. It's the kind of pop-kitsch thing that refuses to die, but it all seems to make sense in the desert, whether it's Vegas or the Springs. And tonight, it felt like fun.

We breezed through the lobby, past the little black guy who sat riffing on the giant white piano, and made our way out to the pool area, where three men, dressed as Frank, Sammy, and Dino, sang with a nine-piece band, surrounded by couples smoking and sipping wine, Jack Daniels and pricey champagne in the open-air blue-stripe cabanas. Sinatra's doppelganger threw a gesture to the band, and a brassy intro led into "This Town," which felt a bit mean-spirited, self-flagellating, and somehow extraordinarily appropriate for this crowd, which was mostly skimpily attired in their naughtiest beachwear... unless they were in evening dresses and jackets with ties. The severe desert heat was mellowing, but only slightly, so the pools were filling with amorous bathers as they climbed atop the big canvas-covered blue floats and made waves as they got frisky.

"What do you want to drink?" Toni asked.

"How about a real girl drink, like a Brandy Alexander?"

"Ooh, Old School! I like it!" She turned to the bartender, cutting in front of a long line of patrons waiting their turn at the bar. "Two Brandy Alexanders, please!" The bartender, young and blonde and wearing a black T-shirt and board shorts, was happy to serve us, the interlopers, despite the complaints from the people waiting in line behind us. Toni held the drinks high as we squeezed through the dancers, then handed me mine as she sipped at hers.

"Oh, hell, fuck being dainty," she said as she slammed the drink and tossed the plastic cup over her head. I chose to sip mine, but it didn't take long for it to disappear.

The beat was as sultry as the night air, and supple bodies in bikinis and board shorts were shiny with perspiration as they danced in rhythm. Dancers surrounded the pools, and the scent of sex was beside the point. Toni dragged me into the throbbing crowd and started to dance with her typical girlish abandon. I felt awkward and out of place here, embarrassed and clumsy.

"Come *on*, Chase! Dance!"

"I feel stupid," I curmudgeoned.

"Me, too!" she answered. "Isn't it great?"

She grabbed both my hands and she started to swing me. It didn't take long before I started to feel the cocktail ignited by the music, and I started to swing and sway on my own. Once I was grabbed by the rhythm, Toni swung away from me and started dancing with the guy behind her, which by this time was fine with me. The music was swingy and great and had taken hold of me, and I had no problem dancing on my own. Toni had been consumed by the crowd of dancers by now, deep in the belly of the beast, but I was happy to be out here on the sidelines, right near the band, feeling the blast of the horn section lighting up the night. Guys would come up to me and start dancing in front of me, but I was happy to be on my own, with my eyes closed, my drink long gone, and "Fly Me to the Moon" stringing me along.

When next I opened my eyes, I found them fixed on Little Sinatra, who was staring right at me. There was nothing subtle about his gaze, and I resented it at first: yeah, the singer in the band choosing his playmate for the night. But to be honest, he really had a great voice, and his look, though it strove for seduction, was really a little bit shy... at least, it seemed so to me. It was like he was expected to use that come-hither look with the ladies, but a little embarrassed to exercise it. He was slender and a little too tall for Frank, I realized, and when he took off the stupid hat, he really looked nice. His eyes were Sinatra-blue, as well, and I could tell they weren't contacts. There were pools of sweat ringing his armpits under the blue Sy Devore jacket, and he was selling that song for all it was worth. For me. It was really sort of cute.

I hadn't felt that little pulse of attraction in a long time. Yes, there was that one time on *Frankel's People*, and I blush to even think about it. Thank God it was just a guest star and not a regular, but I can't believe I let myself give in to it. Jimmy and I had been having our "problems" for about a year by then, and I guess I was just vulnerable. I'd never gone for the Pretty Boys, even back in high school, but I was lonely and hurting and when someone that good-looking and that gentle and that sweet gives you so much time and energy, and when we ran lines together at his apartment on Barrington on the other end of town, well, it now seems so obvious and inevitable that I cringe when I remember it. The lines were memorized by eight, but they'd be rewritten before the next morning. In series television, you can never count on the text you're studying; there's a roomful of writers and producers who have to work their egos into every episode.

We knew the text wasn't important; we knew, as well, why we really were together that night at his place. I allowed myself to be seduced, knowing that I was just another in a long line of conquests for this Hollywood Bowflex Commando. I was a married woman, but I hadn't felt married for a long time. At the end of the night, my ass in a cooling puddle of dysfunctional, unsatisfying coupling, I regretted it all. I was glad when the episode ended, and we moved on to the next guest star. That was the one and only time I stepped out of my miserable marriage and into another man's bed, and in hindsight, it was worse than the miserable marriage. I haven't heard from him since, though he was nominated for an Emmy last year on *CSI: Miami*. He lost.

So here I danced, feeling heat in my loins for the first time in I can't remember how long, sharing a trance with a Sinatra impersonator. It felt tawdry, to say the least, but my level of self-respect was at an all-time low. If this were 1956, and the real Frank Sinatra were making ring-a-ding eyes at me, singing like the song was written for me, surely I would have wilted in his embrace. Or would I? But this young, athletic-looking version of Frank-Through-the-Looking-Glass and I were sharing hormonal desire that could only lead in one direction. Well, the band reached the moon, and Pseudo-Dean Martin grabbed the mike from Frank, and started belting out "Everybody Loves Somebody." It was goofy and cornball and played for all its camp value, but the crowd started slow-dancing together anyway. It was as good an excuse as any.

Without even so much as a look back at his band, Frank left the bandstand, and came right for me. "May I have this dance?" he asked me, with 1950s politeness. I wanted to resist, but the Brandy Alexander didn't. I guess when you're unhappy, it doesn't take much. So I let him take my hand and put his arms around me.

He was a pretty good dancer: a hell of a lot better than me. I was happy to let him lead. His hands lay gently on my shoulders, and as our bodies pressed together, warmer even than the Palm Springs night, I let them caress my bare back. It felt good to be in a man's arms again. Though his dancing was smooth, his seduction was tentative. His hands never dropped lower than the middle of my back, and, without thinking, I allowed my head to rest at the base of his neck. I could smell his sweat overwhelming the antiperspirant, but it was a masculine, welcome musk. I fit pretty nicely against him. This was so unlike me. Physical intimacy has to work its way through a padlocked barricade for me, and takes lots of time and patience. I don't normally like to be touched, but this sweltering night found me somehow needy, emptier than usual, and this good-looking, talented singer dancing me gently across the concrete lip of the Riviera's swimming pool, under the approving influence of a couple of cocktails and the seductive music of another era, was melting me.

The crowd had quieted as the music had slowed, and it was easy for me to be mesmerized. I opened my eyes to look up at the wash of stars through the palm fronds as a gentle breeze kissed me. I felt relaxed in a way I hadn't in a couple years. I looked out at the sea of dancers, all of them held in thrall by a journey into the past, dancing together, some of them kissing, most of them smiling. But one dark face stood out, and my heart thumped me out of my reverie. Halfway across the concrete dancefloor, Jaxon-with-an-X was glaring at me.

"What's the matter?" Frank asked me.

"Nothing. I'm okay."

"You sure?"

Of course I wasn't, but I said I was. I looked back into the crowd, but my lunchbox fan was nowhere to be seen.

The song ended to quiet applause, and it was time for the band to take a break. I looked through the crowd, wondering what had happened to Toni. I couldn't see her anywhere. I had lost track of Jaxon, as well.

"Can I buy you a drink?" Frank asked.

I couldn't think of a reason to decline, so I didn't.

"A Brandy Alexander for the lady," he told the bartender, not having to wait in line.

TEN

When I got home from the funeral, the house felt as empty as I did. I threw my black jacket onto the back of the couch and walked into the kitchen. I opened the refrigerator and just stared at its contents, forgetting what I was doing there. My stomach soured as I looked at the heat-and-eat packages from Whole Foods. I wasn't hungry, I wasn't thirsty, I was psychically evacuated. I looked around the kitchen; all of the flowers that had cheered the room before were browning and shriveled. In my head, I imagined the same thing happening to Chase inside that closed coffin. I left the kitchen and made my way to my office, the one place not occupied by the ghost of Chase Willoughby.

I turned on the iMac and headed to JustSpotted.com, the celebrity-tracking site, and searched Chase's name. Fortunately, the site tracked even the most minor celebrities, most of them a mystery to me, so it didn't take long to find that Chase had been pegged by some camera-phone stalking fan at Kate Mantilini's in the Valley earlier the night of the murder. The house was closing in on me, stifling me; I could barely breathe. At the funeral, all I wanted was to get home. Once I got there, all I wanted was to get away. So I drove out to Kate Mantilini's for lunch.

It was a quiet afternoon, well, barely even afternoon, so it was early for the lunch crowd. I went to the bar and ordered a JD rocks. I used to drink it a lot in my single days, but when my marriage started going sour, I found that it just made me more melancholy. I figured I couldn't get more melancholy than I was now, so I ordered the next one without the rocks.

It was plain that the raven-haired bartender with the enormous brown eyes knew who I was by the way she avoided my gaze. It was obvious that she was a hopeful actress by her looks, of course, but also by her outgoing manner with all the other customers. She kept her charm at a remove from me, knowing she had nothing to gain here. But a trace of sympathy made its way through her officiousness; I had lost my wife, after all, even if I was an asshole.

She kept herself busy polishing the opposite end of the bar, hoping that Shawn Ryan or Ryan Murphy or some other more important Ryan might pull up a stool and settle in.

"Excuse me," I called down the length of the bar. She looked up, but kept her distance.

"You sure you want a refill?"

I held up my current drink, still half-full, to show her I was content in the drink department.

"Were you here when Chase Willoughby came in for dinner the other night?"

A shiver seemed to run up her spine, and she shook her head, going slightly pale. "I work days."

"Do you know who waited on her?"

"That was Danny. He already talked to the big detective."

"I'm not a cop," I told her.

"I know who you are," she told me back. "I'm sorry for your loss. Your wife was beautiful. She used to come in a lot."

"Yeah, sometimes with me."

Our conversation stalled for a moment.

"Is Danny working here today?"

"He works nights. Though he hasn't been in since… well… since that night. He was pretty upset when he heard about it on the news. We all were. We really liked her."

As opposed to you was left unsaid, but I knew how to fill in the blanks.

"Is there a way I could get Danny's number?"

"No, I don't think I can do that."

I grabbed a napkin and a pen, and scribbled my number on it.

"Here, give him my number and ask him to call me. It's important. I need to know what happened to my wife."

"And you don't trust the police?"

"Would you?"

She didn't answer, but she did take my number and put it in her pocket.

Ω Ω Ω

Opening a "Who Killed Chase Willoughby" Facebook page was either the best or the worst idea I'd ever had, but I was at a literal dead end. Lacking any kind of evidence to work from, other than a corpse, her presumed pubic hair, and her unanswered calls to my wife's mobile phone, I didn't know where to turn next. The police, in LA and Arizona, would conduct their investigations at their own speed, alongside hundreds of other cases that demanded their attention as well. I might as well get the Great Unwashed involved to do some of that legwork for me. So I opened the account and offered $100,000 to any information leading to the capture and conviction of whoever the fuck killed my wife. Obviously, I didn't have that kind of money in the bank, but I'd find a way to get it, even if it had to be from SAG insurance. It didn't take long before the site attracted traffic; obviously, people were searching Chase Willoughby and ending up here. "Fans" and "likes" started racking up immediately, in startling numbers, along with private messages from every crackpot admirer and dreamer, every amateur Sherlock Holmes and loose cannon would-be psychiatrist.

Still, I had to look at every message, hoping beyond hope that a clue would come from the outside, anonymous world. The messages came flying in, but most of them were obvious creeps, typing messages from Mommy's basement in deplorable grammar, everything from love notes to "she got what she deserved." It was assumed that if you were a celebrity, then the public owned you, claimed purchase to your life rights in perpetuity. They deserved to control your life, you were there to please them, and if you crossed them, they would reject you, ostracize you, hate you to the point that you deserved to die. Here was a woman known for being a precocious and beautiful young teenager, and she drew such invective from outraged Christians for having been impregnated by an Older Man that she deserved to be immolated in the deepest chambers of Hell. Lots of notes on how beautiful and charming she was, but practically as many about what a shitty actress she was. Human beings are fickle, self-centered, detestable creatures sometimes.

There was communication from within the Hollywood community, as well. More reality show producers tried to make contact here, the real low-end bottom-feeders from channels I'd never heard of. Or the Hollywood hopefuls who just knew they had the right take to attach their leechy, fanged suckermouths to Chase Willoughby and ride her cadaver to fame and fortune.

But as for meaningful clues? Maybe later, certainly not now.

My eyes were red and burning; I hadn't looked away from the screen in hours. When I did look up, I saw that the August sun was setting, shrouding itself in pink and purple clouds. My head was throbbing, and I pressed my palms against my eyes, suddenly aware of the dull, thudding ache. Then, the phone in my pocket began to ring. I pulled it out to check the caller ID, but it just read "blocked". I answered anyway.

"Mr. Willoughby?"

I guess that's who I'll be until the day I die.

"Close enough," I answered.

"This is Danny Reed, the waiter from Kate Mantilini? Delores told me you wanted me to call you?"

"Danny, hi!" I couldn't believe it. His voice was lilty, like some sort of gay caricature on *South Park* or something. "Thank you for calling me back. Listen, I'd love to talk to you about the night my wife was there."

"Delores told you I'd already spoken with the police, didn't she?"

"She did. But this has nothing to do with the police. I just need to know what happened to Chase. Maybe you can help. Where do you live? I can come to you…"

"No, not my place. Do you know Aroma, on Tujunga in Studio City?"

"I know it. Meet you there in an hour or so?"

There was a long hesitation.

"Okay. At about nine, right?"

"Good. I'll see you then."

I didn't know what would come of this, but at least it seemed like some sort of progress.

Ω Ω Ω

Aroma is a cute outdoor coffee house and café on one short, charming block of Studio City, sort of halfway between the CBS Studios and Universal City. The coffee and tea drinks were good, and the desserts elaborate and expansively caloric. Almost all of the seating was outside in a jumble of mismatched tables and chairs, under a canopy of oaks and elm. Its sweetness, however, meant that there was always an endless line for service that snaked out the door and down the street. It was a popular hangout for out-of-work actors and writers and TV weathermen. It was a rare table that didn't sport a pile of trade papers and a clattering MacBook Air, and the atmosphere was always charged with chatter about The Industry. The place was particularly photogenic at night, when the strings of little white lights wrapped around the trees were ablaze. It was probably ninety degrees or so on this night, and the crowd was dressed accordingly, sipping iced lattes and scooping the last melting remains of Italian ice cream from the tiny cups they'd gotten from the gelato place a few doors down. At least a couple dozen of the patrons had their fashionable dogs with them, which acted as magnets for the opposite sex.

I had no idea what young Mr. Reed looked like, but I figured he'd know me, so I just sat on the bench out in front and waited for him to arrive. Soon I felt the sensation of eyes on me. It seemed like any time I looked up, someone was just looking away. Call it paranoia if you like, but I know that I was being recognized in the only way I would ever achieve any sort of fame: as the husband of the slaughtered TV star. Before long, the people around me didn't even bother to hide their glances. I felt I was living in a scene directed by Roman Polanski.

I was relieved when the thin, frosted-haired young man with the pierced, drooping earlobes in the white tennis shorts and matching immaculately pressed short-sleeved shirt and pink Crocs walked nervously up to me. He was holding a shivering little Italian Greyhound cradled in one arm: shivering despite the ninety-degree heat. It looked as nervous as its owner.

"Mr. Willoughby, sorry I'm late." He reached out with a trembling hand to shake.

"It's Turrentine, actually, but just call me James. Can I call you Danny?"

"Of course. I'm sorry. I'm so embarrassed."

"Don't worry about it; it's not the first time anybody made that mistake. What can I get you?"

"Iced soy chai latte?" he ventured.

"Great. Pick us a table, and I'll find you." ‑

The spot he snagged happened to be tiny, and right next to a long table filled with young thespians. Acting class must have just gotten out, as the entire group was engaged in theoretical approaches to representing the human condition. From the Russian stage to three-camera sitcom technique, from Stanislavsky to Roy London, from improvisation to the Method, they argued amongst themselves as if it really mattered how they played the third Terrorist from the right or the guy in the Fruit of the Loom grape costume. It just made me tired.

I handed Danny his chai latte, and settled into the uncomfortable wrought-iron chair that seemed to have daggers pointed at the center of my back.

"Thank you, Mr. Turrentine," said the polite young Danny.

"James, please. Thank you for meeting me, Danny. So far as I can tell, you're the last one to see my wife before she… before she, you know…"

His eyes were filling with tears, and the little Iggy he held so close was licking at his face, its long legs looped over his arm.

"She was a beautiful woman," he practically sobbed. I nodded in agreement, hating the use of the past tense.

"Was she alone that night?"

"Oh, no! She was with the little redhead, like I told the policeman. The other one who was, um, killed. Didn't they tell you that?"

As a matter of fact, they didn't.

"Of course. Besides her," I said.

"No, just the two of them. It was a ladies' night out, they said."

"So they seemed happy?"

"Very happy! Like girlfriends out for a night on the town. Your wife even had the porterhouse!"

I'd never seen Chase eat a mammal, as long as I've known her.

"I gave her a crème brûlée, but don't tell the manager."

"So they were cheerful, then."

"Absolutely, that's the exact word. Very cheerful."

"Did they talk about where they were going?"

"Just that they were going out, a night on the town, I think, is exactly what they said."

"But they didn't mention a place?"

He really wanted to have an answer for me, but he didn't. His eyes were glassy with unspilled tears. He just shook his head.

"I feel just terrible about this, Mr.—James. I want so much to help. I just don't know anything else." He pulled a lace hand-kerchief out of his pocket, like something my grandmother might have given for Christmas, and blew his neatly shaved nose. "I haven't been able to go back to work since... since that night."

I watched him suffer, wondering how he could feel so deeply about someone he'd only served one night in a restau-rant, amazed by the power of television and celebrity.

"And they just took off after dinner? No mention of any destination, a club or anything? Nothing you might have overheard, even if they weren't talking to you?"

He was quiet for a moment, as if wondering whether he should divulge a secret between the girls.

"The only thing I heard Chase say was that she wanted to go someplace nobody knew her. But I don't know if that helps."

I nodded.

"Neither do I." We sat in silence, as the beautiful, hopeful young people at the table next to us with bright eyes, perfect skin, and high hopes chattered incessantly about their future stardom. I didn't want to be the one to tell them the truth; I'd ruined enough lives by now. Danny looked ready to leave, and I could see there was nothing more to learn here, about Chase's death or about life in general.

"And there's nothing at all you can think of that you might have overheard? It's not rude or disloyal, you know. It might be helpful."

He actually squirmed, but that could have been due to the wrought-iron seating as much as any inner turmoil.

"Anything at all..."

"I passed by them quickly when I left her a crème brûlée. I thought I heard the redhead say something about the desert, though it might have been dessert."

The desert! The fucking desert! It reared its ugly, sandy head again.

When I got up, the metal legs of the chair made a horrendous squeal across the rough concrete floor, bringing the thespianic chatter at the next table to an abrupt, annoyed halt. "Thanks, Danny. I really appreciate it."

I gulped down the dregs of my mocha caramel latte, and left him with his alien little bug-eyed dog, which he let drink chai from his cup.

Ω Ω Ω

When I pulled up in my driveway at about ten o'clock, two vehicles were waiting for me: a navy blue Crown Victoria and an Arizona Highway Patrol cruiser. Sitting in the bentwood rockers on my porch, facing one another, were Detective Maldonado and Sheriff Hardy. I feared for the future of Maldonado's chosen seat, as it groaned under his massiveness. There must have been a sale on that suit, either that or it was the only one he had. But it was sharp, and helped define his indefinably squishy girth. It felt as if he could not exist without the suit, that if you opened it up, he would spill out into a giant puddle of Maldonado at your feet. In it, he had power, shape, function. Hardy, on the other hand, was invincibly defined, exercised and physical, despite the smoldering Lucky Strike in his mouth. His summer uniform shirt fit him tightly, exposing imposing biceps. And yet, given a choice between whom I'd rather go up against, I'd choose Hardy any day. I got the feeling that Maldonado, despite his beefiness and quiet manner, could be ruthless, even deadly.

They stood as I came up the walk from the driveway.

I waved away the smoke from Hardy's cigarette. "I'd appreciate it if you didn't smoke right in front of my house."

Hardy dropped the cigarette and ground it out with his foot... on my doorstep.

"That's what I told him," Maldonado said. "Those fucking things will kill you. Killed my dad, killed his dad, too. Just started growing fat around his heart, slowing it down; kept killing Pop for about eight years before he finally passed." He took a sip off his Jamba Juice smoothie, as Hardy put out his fire with something from Starbucks. Hardy threw a glare at the LA detective. Seemed like some sort of competition was going on here.

"Can this wait until morning?" I asked. "I'm really tired."

"That makes three of us," Maldonado offered. "Yeah, it can wait until morning, but I'd rather it didn't."

"I have to get back to Phoenix as soon as I can," said Hardy.

Maldonado smiled at me, but there was no joy in his grin. "We hear you've been playing cop."

I was in no mood to be put on the defensive. I could see faces peering from peek-a-boo curtains across the street.

"Maybe we should take this inside," Hardy said.

"Excellent idea," Maldonado agreed. So I unlocked the door and let them in.

Maldonado took in the whole place as he entered, though Hardy's attention was just on myself.

"Cute place," Maldonado said with enthusiasm. "Not big, but cozy. Artsy. I was expecting one of those big, modern places with no personality, you know, one of those cavernous Bauhaus things they have all over the hills, all architecture, no humanity. This place feels lived-in, inhabited."

"I'm glad you approve," I said.

Maldonado frowned. "No need to be sarcastic. I was giving you a compliment."

"Sorry," I said, but I wasn't. "Thank you."

"It is a very nice place," Hardy said, not wanting to feel left out.

"Mind if we sit?" Maldonado asked, as he settled onto the blue velvet sofa like Jabba the Hut. "I'm carrying a bit of a load."

"Please." Hardy remained on his feet. "Sheriff?"

"I'll stand, thanks."

"Suit yourself."

"I'm not usually this big; I've been on cortisone treatments, and it's blown me up like a balloon. You wouldn't believe how little I eat."

I didn't know what to say to that: I'm sorry? So I took a seat in the Stickley opposite the officers of the law.

Maldonado nodded to Hardy, making it clear who was in the power seat here. "Why don't you start, Tom?"

I thought I saw Hardy's jaw tighten in resentment.

"Thanks." Hardy turned to me and away from the big guy. "Mr. Turrentine, did you know Antoinette McLoughlin?"

I turned to see Maldonado huff, and his body shuffled on the couch. "We've been over this with Mr. Turrentine, Tom. I had you copied on our report."

"Thanks, Paul, but I'd like to handle my investigation in my own way."

Maldonado lifted his hand magisterially, turning away. "Sorry."

"Could you answer the question, Mr. Turrentine?"

"No," I told him. "I didn't know her. But I found out that she worked on Chase's last series, *Frankel's People*. I saw her in the cast-and-crew photo." Maldonado nodded, like he already knew this.

"But you don't know if they were friends?"

"No."

"Close friends?"

"I'm not sure what you mean." Oh, yes I was.

"Were they lovers?" Hardy's face was expressionless, all business, but Maldonado was smiling.

"No. Chase didn't go that way."

"To your knowledge."

"To my knowledge and beyond. We've been very open about our sexual pasts with one another, Sheriff. Chase had real problems with intimacy with anyone. She had a lot of... of... issues; it took a lot to get through to her, to get close to her. The likelihood that she had a female lover is just, well, it's just unimaginable to me." I'm such a liar. I can imagine it all too well. My heart was pounding against my ribcage, trying to get out.

"Can you imagine any reason someone might have to kill your wife?"

"Honestly? No. Everybody liked my wife."

"Except you, we hear." Maldonado couldn't keep from contributing to the interrogation. I slowly turned to him.

"What are you saying?" I asked him.

"You told me yourself that you were going through a tough patch in your marriage, right?"

"Yes. But it doesn't mean I killed her."

"Nobody said you killed her."

"Then what are you here for?"

"An education," Maldonado said, sucking the last of his smoothie through the straw with an annoying sputter.

"So you think I killed her."

"Personally?" Maldonado looked wide-eyed and innocent. "No. Like I told you, you don't have it in you. Look, this is an obvious crime of passion, and passion is something I don't think you have much of. But beyond that... I've done this shit for a lot of years, and people are murdered in many ways by many types. I mean, I could be wrong, but you are not one of those types. My friend here from Arizona? He thinks maybe you had something to do with it, like maybe you hired someone to make the hit, but me, I think he's going through the moves, I don't think he really, *truly* believes that, do you Tom?"

Hardy looked like he wanted to kill Maldonado. And I didn't blame him.

"Because I know in my heart of hearts that you didn't. Could I be wrong? Yeah, it's happened before. But I've got a great sense of smell, even with the cortisone treatments, and I don't smell her death on you."

I couldn't tell if this was some kind of tactic, that he was making it seem like an insult to me that I was such a weenie that I was incapable of killing my wife. It was like he was saying *'fraid not!* so that I would say *'fraid so!*

Meanwhile, Hardy was blushing. His investigation had just been scuttled by an overbearing, overweight hot-shot LAPD detective, and now he had to try to justify his existence here. It was a huge tactical mistake for him to have attached his inquiry to Maldonado's. The LA detective just wanted to humiliate the backwater Arizona rube in front of his Hollywood friends.

Hardy was trying unsuccessfully to keep his cool. "You know what? I'm done here. Paul, it's your turn, okay? Thanks for your cooperation, Mr. Turrentine." And he left in the proverbial huff. Maldonado watched him go, then turned to me with a smile. No words, just a smile. In a moment, there was a timid knock on the door. I crossed the room to answer it, and a red-faced Hardy stood there. He looked past me to Maldonado.

"You're blocking my car," he said, and Maldonado took his sweet time rising from the couch and making his way out the door.

Vehicles moved and Hardy's cruiser rumbling away, Maldonado returned, his step more sprightly, and stood appraisingly in the middle of the living room.

"This really is a beautiful little place you've got here."

"Thanks. It's really Chase's taste. She did it all."

"Oh, it's obviously the woman's touch. Still, sweet."

He just looked at it, took it all in. I kept waiting for him to get to the point.

"Is there anything else I can do for you, Detective?"

He turned to me, as if startled out of his reverie.

"Sorry? Oh, no, I just wanted to get a look around, get a sense of who this Wonder Woman was. I have yet to hear a negative word about her. I don't think I've ever met anyone who was so well-loved; shit, I didn't know they existed. Unless you have contradictory testimony you'd like to present?"

Was he goading me or teasing me?

"No," I told him. "Even when we didn't get along, it wasn't her fault." I knew that was true. I knew that I wore the black hat. "She was a genuinely good human being."

"So I hear." He started to walk across the room, his back to me. "Mind if I just look around?"

Did it matter? "Help yourself," I said. And he did.

I followed him as he wandered down the hallway, peeking into the kitchen, and finally into Chase's bedroom. Ornate costumes hung from clothing trees that surrounded the old wooden wardrobe, and he lifted each one, checking them out, nodding approval. He looked at the pictures on the walls and on the dresser.

"No pictures of the two of you together," he noted. I stayed silent. "I'm guessing you have separate rooms? Sorry, 'had'." I nodded, and he just started humming a little song. He smelled her pillow, smiled, then left the bedroom, heading back down the hall. I felt like a puppy as I followed in his wake.

He stepped into Chase's studio and turned on the light.

"I'd heard she was an artist," he said, squinting at her works. "Hm. She was very talented, wasn't she?"

"Yes. She was."

"Big fan of Edvard Munch, wasn't she?"

"I guess so."

"Creepy stuff. Gets under your skin, doesn't it? Get the feeling she wasn't very happy." He turned and looked directly at me for that last bit. All I could do was shrug.

"Mind if I take a look at your bedroom?"

"Be my guest."

"You can say no if you want. I don't have a search warrant or anything."

"I've got nothing to hide."

"I know," he grinned. "I'm just fucking with you." He led me out of Chase's studio, and I led him up the stairs and into my room.

He entered, still nodding, as if this was just what he expected. "Yep, pretty Spartan. Not much of a woman's touch in here, is there?" I assumed the question was rhetorical. So after a cursory glance or two, he turned, forgetting he was a fat man, and tripped gingerly down the stairs and into the living room.

"Thanks, Jim," he said, as if he had gathered a ton of damning evidence. "I appreciate your cooperation. I think that's all I need for now. I'll call you. And you've got my card, right? Just in case you need to reach me directly?"

"I do."

"Good. Sweet dreams." And then he was gone.

I watched through the window as he pulled away, and the house settled into unbroken quietude, leaving me to wonder what the fuck that was all about.

$$\Omega \; \Omega \; \Omega$$

I went right to my office, and awakened the iMac. I went directly to the new Facebook page, and there were already close to a hundred new messages since last I looked. I pored over them, and it was just more bullshit, fawning or raving or loving or hating, anonymous blather about a beautiful girl that the world thought they knew because they had shared her on their TVs. One misspelled message after another, deaf, dumb and blind, each trying to connect itself with the doused flame of celebrity. I was just about to shut it down and go to bed when one message heading jumped out and wrapped its fingers around my neck:

I saw her in the desert.

It was from somebody who called himself Jumbo Jax.

My hands started to shake as I opened his message, knowing it would take me back to heat and sand and mesquite and cactus and blood and death.

I saw her, the message said, *out in the desert. If you're telling the truth about the reward, contact me privately.*

I sent him a message that very moment, and sat waiting for a couple hours before I gave up and went to bed.

ELEVEN

I didn't even like Brandy Alexanders, to tell you the truth. I didn't much care for alcohol at all. But on this night, they tasted like a milkshake, and I felt warm inside and out. My Imitation Sinatra felt like the real thing, and he was so sweet and solicitous and engagingly shy that I felt surprisingly comfortable in his presence. Before long, I was at least as comfortable in his arms.

I'd caught a glimpse of Toni at the far side of the crowd; she hopped up and down to wave at me, throwing me the okay sign when she saw me dancing with Frank. But I'd forgotten about her by now. The band was done for the moment, replaced by a girl trio, and Frank, who had his own band and wrote his own songs, had shed Old Blue Eyes for the night. His real name was Riley, and they were listening to his new demo at Universal right now, and his hopes were high. He loved the Sinatra gig because it gave him a swagger he didn't really possess. When he was Frank, he told me, he was all those things he couldn't be in his own body: confident, funny, sexy, popular. Beneath the costume, he was shy, a mind hopelessly trapped in a body, an artist. His first kiss was tentative, exploratory, and I felt that I needed to take the lead: me, the married woman, the tower of ice, the lady locked behind the gate. So I kissed him, held his head in my hands, stroked his cheek, tasted his breath.

This couldn't be a good idea.

But that didn't stop me, and neither did Riley. Or Frank.

When we ended up in his room, lying on his bed, clothes lying pathetically on the too-authentic red shag hotel carpeting, I came to my senses. There was no way I should be here. Yes, it felt good to be held, to be kissed, to be desired, but it opened wounds that had hidden behind the desert air and the alcohol. The chilly breeze from the rattling window-box air conditioner woke me up, and—dressed in nothing but gooseflesh, pressed against his taut young body—I pulled away.

"What is it?" he asked.

"I am so fucked up," I said, pulling the sheet over me.

To his credit, he didn't try to pull me back.

"No," he said. "You're beautiful."

His gaze was so appreciative that it was almost loving, not lascivious, despite the flush of color across his cheeks. I held the sheet in front of me, and he didn't try to take it away. He didn't try to do anything. He had no idea who I was, and that made it harder. I could have been Kathy or Vanessa or Jayne or Linda, and it wouldn't have made any difference to him. But I was Chase. The name of a bank. That's all he knew.

"I don't feel beautiful," I told him.

"Well then, I know better than you do. So your opinion is thrown out of court."

"I shouldn't be here."

"Yes, you should."

I stood in the middle of the tawdry little room, the mirrored sliding closet doors reflecting me into repetitious oblivion in the mirror above the dresser. There were no lights; there was no camera; there would be no action.

"It's not right."

"It felt pretty right a couple minutes ago."

I looked at him and nodded. It did. So what was I beating myself up over? My marriage? Was it being unfaithful if your marriage was a prison? All of the passion and lust that had been fueled by the drinks and the shy, pretty, talented young singer who only came to life in the costume of another came crashing down on me in a sudden revelation: I did not exist. I was a character in a play, whose happiness was shoved back into a dark and hidden chamber between performances. Life and happiness and family and fulfillment were only truly available to me when I played a part. Those real-life moments in between imploded into a denial of existence, a hollowness that tried to scream itself to life on mediocre canvases in my studio. So here I was again, live onstage at the Riviera, Chase Willoughby, with thrilling co-star Frank Sinatra, in *Palm Springs Romance*! I felt the curtain come crashing down, and my desire leaked out, puddling beneath me at my feet. I had eaten another soul and spit it out.

Tears formed in my eyes and Frank—*Riley*—walked over to me, still naked, shameless, and wrapped his arms around me.

"You don't have to stay here if you don't want to," he whispered in my ear. "I want you here—I *really* want you here—but I'm not going to make you stay."

The tears came harder. I knew I wouldn't be crying if it weren't for the drinks; hell, I wouldn't be in this fucking boho hotel room if it hadn't been for the drinks. But here I was, and here I was crying in the arms of a stranger. He kissed me softly on the cheek.

I sniffed and wiped the back of my arm across my flooded eyes, knowing I had to look like some kind of raccoon by now. I gently peeled myself out of his arms and started climbing back into my clothes.

"I'm sorry," I told him over and over. "I'm so sorry."

"Me, too," Riley said, sitting on the corner of his bed and watching me dress. He looked it.

After I stepped back into my dress and my shoes, he asked if I needed him to zip me up… but I was done. There was no zipper. My back was bare.

I didn't want to have to say that if this were a different time and a different place, things might have been different, that he seemed sweet and funny and desirable to me. But then I'd have to tell him all the other stuff, that my life was a train wreck, that I was incapable of love and marriage, that I snuffed out all life around me. I don't think he'd have liked that at all. And neither would I.

So I just kept apologizing and thanking him for being so understanding. And then, leaving him sitting naked on his hotel bed, I left.

Ω Ω Ω

The party was still in swing when I came back out into the night. I had forgotten about the heat until I stepped back into it and it robbed me of my breath. The music was sprightly and the crowd loopy and inebriated; the scent of lust and date palms baked and simmered. My little clutch purse in hand, I roamed the dancefloor, seeking but not finding Toni. Men grabbed at me, tried to pull me into their mating dance, but I was on a mission, and this missionary was not interested in social intercourse. I had to find my ride and get home before curfew.

But Toni, the chipper little leprechaun life of the party, was nowhere to be found. Perhaps she had found solace and romance in one of those very rooms into which I had been granted a peek. Perhaps she was making the beast with two backs under the mirrors to the hushed, panting musings of "Fever", soaking the percales with sweat and perfume. I wondered if she were bedded down with man or woman. Or maybe she had just not been able to find me, and left the Riviera to find her sad-sack friend.

I didn't want to interrupt her pleasure, but needed to make sure that my ride was still around. I needed to call her. I reached into my purse for my phone, but it was gone. Shit! I never forget my phone! But this night, somehow my lifeline had gone missing. I didn't even have Toni's number, but certainly I could look it up. If I had a phone with me, that is. And I didn't. I just kept looking for her, but the options were running out. Finally, having covered every searchable inch of the Riviera's public nightlife, I took a cab back to Palm Canyon Drive, hoping that her bright red hair would call out to me.

The street was filled with summer foot traffic, the night still sultry and inviting. I walked through the walking dead, not knowing where the hell to look next. If nothing else, I could go to the parking lot and just wait at her car. Surely before long she would find me missing and know where we should meet. Perhaps she was looking for me even now.

So I went to the garage in the high hopes of finding tiny Toni waiting there for me, but I could not have been more wrong. Her little Mini was gone.

Ω Ω Ω

Now what?

I stood in the empty parking slot in the sweltering, three-story concrete structure, wondering what I should do. Surely Toni was driving around searching for me, right? There weren't that many places to hide here in the Springs; there was Palm

Canyon Drive and… what else? If I kept walking the main drag, surely she would spot me and we'd compare notes and laugh and make fun of ourselves and tootle back to Los Angeles and greet the sunrise over smoothies at Lulu's Beehive.

But what if her car was stolen? What if something happened to her?

And why would she have taken her car away in the first place?

I went back around the corner and onto Palm Canyon. The wind kicked up a bit harder, and some dry, brittle fronds from the high palms lining the street crashed at my feet, making me jump. Dates pelted me. A pink Corvette convertible screeched around the corner, one of its hubcaps choosing that moment to break free, bouncing noisily up onto the sidewalk and across my feet, rattling as it tumbled to a stop against a big green trashcan. No one else seemed to notice, but my nerves were on edge. The night and its attendant demons were turning on me. Beelzebub stood with pitchfork in hand, waiting for me around every corner.

Okay, I'm dramatic. I'm an actress, right?

I was feeling suddenly alone, alone in ways that I was used to at home, but not on this night. This was a night meant to put a Band-Aid over all that loneliness, to remind me how to smile. Instead, I was starting to get scared.

I stumbled past Las Casuelas, where the night had begun. The aging, pot-bellied, balding classic rockers were putting heart and soul into some horrible, strangled Doobie Brothers song, and a red-faced woman, pinched into toreador pants that were a couple sizes too small for her, lurched up her night's ration of margaritas all over her bloodshot, Hawaiian-shirted date. Their dream dance had come to an end.

Somehow the bright, colorful lights of the night seemed to be getting brighter, an iris opening as if to another dimension. Whites got whiter, hotter, searing, and I could see deeper into the shadows. I knew what this signaled, and I fought against the onslaught of the pain I knew I would have to endure. If the migraines found me here, I would be at their mercy. I tried to build a wall around my brain.

I watched the slow-motion cluster-fuck of vehicles make their way down the one-way avenue, no place to go, really, but needing to be out in the night air, anyway. No sign of the Mini, of Toni, of my rescuer. I stumbled past the Follies Theater, where geriatric singers and dancers who once had careers that only people older than them remember pulled on their tights and silk tuxedos and performed boogie-woogie hits from the good old days that weren't really all that good. The first show was letting out, and the sidewalk was blocked with wheelchairs, walkers, and oxygen tanks. I felt like Kevin McCarthy, dying to shout out to them, "They're here! They're already here!" But I kept my silence and squeezed passed the wheezing minions.

Dust devils whirled around me and threw sand in my eyes. I stumbled past the library and crossed the street, colliding into two pudgy gay men with matching diamond ear studs, spilling their massive Bloody Marys from Pinocchio's all over us. Funny how *they* kept apologizing to *me* and offering to buy me a drink. I was happy to let them accept responsibility, but I declined the libation. I stood on the corner as the creatures of the night swarmed around me in clusters. My chest drenched with the sticky red beverage, I looked as if a knife had been plunged deep into my heart and I was covered in my own blood.

Calm down, I urged myself. *It's no big deal. Toni will pull up any second now and you'll climb in her car and she'll tell you about*

*the amazing guy or girl she hooked up with and how she just left
him to get back to you and take you home.*

Suddenly, the wind died like a lurching beast that had been
shot through the head. I just closed my eyes and breathed, and
I felt my heartbeat slow down. I wasn't used to feeling like a
damsel in distress. When I started to calm, I opened my eyes,
and the world around me seemed to slow down. I sat at a bench
in front of the Coffee Bean and wiped the sweat from my brow
with the back of my hand. It dried instantly in the dry heat.

The headache was tearing down the wall of Jericho, and I
felt it grow like a burning tumor behind my eyes. I pressed my
palms against my eyes and felt an inch of relief, but I knew it
signaled a pain that would grow and not abate anytime soon.
Fear of the migraine was almost as bad as the migraine itself.

Lub dub, my heart told me. *Lub. Dub.*

Slowing, calming, not pounding my brain so hard. Deep
breaths, no fear, this too shall pass. And it actually started to.
However, my relief proved to be only momentary.

I let my hands drop from my eyes, easing them open and
letting in the lights of the boulevard. It no longer stung; I could
see normally, without the painful intensity that the headaches
brought with them. Not all of the faces that revealed themselves were staring at me, which was a relief. The children of
the desert night were oblivious, maybe even disdainful to me,
the crazy disheveled woman with the sticky red goo making her
green silk Versace stick to her skin. Fine. I was ready for their
backs.

And then:

I saw him seeing me. Jaxon-with-an-X, his unblinking glare
fixed on me, stood under the streetlight across the road, casting
a long shadow, a slash of light across his face illuminating ce-
rulean eyes that tried to stab me. I gasped as he held me snared

in his gaze, frozen, immobilized. When he started to cross the street, ignoring the red light and dancing through the sludgy cross traffic, I bolted like a gazelle stalked by the king of the jungle. He picked up his pace and I ran like hell, pushing pedestrians out of my way as I tumbled through them. He never got faster than a quick walk; I never slowed from a full-on run.

I was not dressed for a chase scene; I ran wobbling on my Ferragamos, and knew it was only a matter of time before a broken heel betrayed me. But I ran for all I was worth, down Tahquitz Canyon Way, foolishly away from the safety of the surrounding—if intoxicated—crowd. I threw a look over my shoulder, and Jaxon was the tortoise, slow and steady, taking his time, knowing how easily he could vanquish a mere woman. I ran like a man, and twisted around onto Indian Canyon drive, seeking a place to hide. The frozen yogurt place disgorged a party of local teenagers just as I passed the open doorway, acting as a blind for me. I lost sight of him then, knowing better than to look back but doing it anyway. I crossed East Andreas, getting further still from the populated center of town, drenched in sweat and the rasp of a parched, dry windpipe. It was the next sudden turn onto East Amado that led to the first broken heel, twisting my ankle with a sudden agonizing tear. I lost my footing and tumbled headfirst against the concrete wall with enough power to make my brain flash. I sat on the sidewalk, hugging the shadows, the arid desert scorching my lungs. My ankle was tender; I tried to stand on it, but it gave out on me, and I fell back to the cement. I tried to control my breathing, will my heart to slow down, but my body had been overtaxed, overpowered by survival mode.

A car passed, headlights wrapping around me and letting me go, returning me to shadow. Only blocks from the bleating, beating heart of the city, Palm Springs revealed itself as the small town it really was. The streets here were nearly deserted. The Mexican restaurant at the corner was already closed. The corner streetlight flickered twice, and then lapsed into darkness. A garden of sparkling quartz gravel lost its glint as it was plunged into night.

I dared to look down Indian Canyon, which was bereft of life, and allowed myself the luxury of breathing. I had escaped. I rested my back against the wall, feeling tears welling in my eyes. I fought them back, refusing to let them spill.

It only took a few short blocks to leave the commercial section of the Springs, and this part of town was alarmingly bleak and silent after the curtain of night had fallen. The appliance repair shop next to the Mexican restaurant had a FOR LEASE sign in the window. The mom and pop video store across the street had long been shuttered. Sitting on the still-hot sidewalk, I took off my shoes and shoved them—or what was left of them—into my purse. Long, low sweat stains painted my dress below my arms, and the spilled Bloody Mary was going stiff as it dried and hardened. Using the wall, I eased myself up into a one-legged stand, testing my swollen ankle. It could almost take my weight, I thought.

Then I heard the only sound since the passing car: a gentle, distant *clip, clip, clip* of shoes: *men's* shoes. I held my breath and dared another peek. Sound carries in the desert, particularly at night, so at first I wasn't sure where it came from. I squinted, as if that would give me the X-ray vision I would need to see into the darkness. As it turned out, it was more than a block away: a man's figure, hands in pockets, its endless shadow shrinking as it drew further from the streetlight behind it was taking its time as it approached. It was Jaxon, and he was coming my way.

I looked in every direction, seeking someplace to hide. Down at the next corner, surrounded by businesses that had given up the ghost long ago and lay fallow and reverently dark, light leaked out of an open door. The simple blue neon letters above the entrance were a beacon: THE CLAMSHELL. I hobbled across the street and down the block, entering the place just as Jaxon rounded the corner. There was no way he didn't see me. I pulled the door shut behind me.

The Clamshell was a tavern, dark to the point of gloomy. k.d. Lang sang a country ballad on the jukebox, and the place was nearly empty. A handful of couples huddled in the corners of the place, and this place was all corners. It was festooned with blowfish and rope nets, cowboy saddles and interstate license plates perforated with bullet holes. The tiny dancefloor had but one brave pair swooning in time to the music, mouths pressed against each other's necks.

The man behind the bar was polishing glasses, dressed in a crisp, white, short-sleeved shirt rolled up to the shoulders, hair slicked back, a gold stud in his right ear, a broken heart tattooed on his swollen bicep, with the word *Jody* broken between its syllables in the rip. I took a seat at the dark end of the bar, the only one occupying a stool, the only one not folded into a clandestine embrace in the nether regions of the tavern.

It was only when the bartender stepped into the red glow of the neon Budweiser sign that I saw that, despite the rough stubble at the base of the chin, he was a she.

"What can I get you, pretty lady?" she asked, her voice surprisingly high and feminine from so masculine a countenance.

"Just a Pellegrino or something," I answered, still out of breath. Another look made me realize that all of the patrons of the Clamshell were women. This night seemed somehow dedicated to Sappho.

"Club soda okay?"

"Fine, thanks."

"Want some extra for the dress?" I looked down to see what a mess I had become. I tried to smile, but it twisted itself into tears instead. Her rough but friendly grin dropped away and grew concerned.

"Somebody's following me…"

At that moment, the door opened, and Jaxon's six-foot silhouette stood tall against the black night. He looked into the place, saw what it was more quickly than I had, and smiled at me.

"You're it," he said.

"Get the fuck outta here," the bartender snarled, her voice dropping a full two octaves.

"Do you know who she is?" Jaxon asked the room, as heads in the shadowy corners turned to me, tiny eyes sparkling from the shaded recesses of the bar.

"I know who she *isn't*, and that's a friend of *yours*. I said get the fuck out." She could have taken him in a dogfight any day.

"Fine." Jaxon flipped her his middle finger, then walked away, letting the door slowly ease shut in his wake.

K.D. wrapped up her sweet, heartbroken song as if on cue, and the little bar went silent. All eyes were on me, but no one spoke. The bartender looked at me, studying me in intimidating silence. I sat awkwardly, pinned under her stare for what seemed like minutes as she searched behind my eyes for something.

"Can I use your phone?" I asked her, and she cocked her head as she stared back at me, studying me as if I were her final exam.

"Who you need to call?"

"A friend."

"Friends are good," she said.

Suddenly, she turned and made her way to the far end of the bar, filled a glass with ice and bubbling water behind her back, squeezed a lime into it, and set it in front of me as a tall, thin blonde with shoulder length hair and a too-prominent nose, wearing faded Lee jeans with deep cuffs and a Dinah Shore Golf Classic T-shirt, crossed the room and dropped a quarter into the vintage Wurlitzer jukebox. Julie London sang "Cry Me a River" and the bartender pulled up a stool across from me, just watching me as I took a sip.

"You okay?" she asked.

"I will be, thanks," I answered.

She picked up an old Princess phone and slammed it onto the bar, just out of my reach, almost as if daring me to use it.

"Frank," she volunteered, extending her hand for me to shake. I reached out hesitantly, and she wrapped her hand tightly around mine. Her palm was calloused, rough, a worker's hand, and her grip was almost painful. I felt weak, soft, vulnerable. She knew it, too, and it made her smile.

"Thank you, Frank," I answered, hoping she didn't notice that I didn't introduce myself in kind.

"It's okay, pretty lady. I know who you are." Not that that gave me comfort. She wouldn't take her eyes off of me, and I squirmed in her appraisal and took another sip. It was bitter, and I guess I made a face.

"What's the matter?" she asked.

"Bitter," I said.

"Must be the lime."

I was getting confused, and the room started to sway, and not just from Julie London. I reached for the phone, but missed.

"You sure this isn't quinine water?" That's what I meant to ask, but it came out thick and mushy. I started to feel like I felt when I was a little girl, alone in bed, about to fall into a dream when the bed starts spinning, and voices started to laugh at me from every direction. My ears started to ring and I could see every minute, sun-damaged crinkle around Frank's eyes. When she smiled, she revealed teeth that were tobacco-stained and filled with cracks and crazes.

Then my face met the floor.

TWELVE

I woke at about six, as the sun reached into my bedroom window and wrapped its invasive tentacles around me. I'd forgotten to shut the blackout curtains. As I rolled over, my stomach howled in protest; I had also forgotten to eat anything for dinner. My eyes felt gritty and swollen, bloodshot from hours at the computer. I threw off the sheet, which was soaked with my perspiration, and climbed into a pair of boxers and a T-shirt. I didn't much care for this dawn shit, but now that I was awake, there wasn't much I could do about it.

I trudged down the hall to my office and, grabbing a Power Bar from my desk drawer, woke the sleeping iMac and went directly to the Facebook page. I scrolled through a couple of pages of fan art, Photoshopped images of Chase's face on angels' bodies, messages of love and loss, hearts and flowers, and noted how most of the haters seemed to have gotten Chase out of their systems by now, and had moved on to other celebrities more deserving of their scorn.

Just when I was about to give up on my new hopeful contact, ready to consign him to the heap of phonies and assholes, Jumbo Jax had posted again, ironically only minutes after I had gone to bed.

Call me at 10 a.m., the message said. Other than the telephone number, which was in the 760 area code, that was it.

Great. I had four hours to waste.

The first thing I did was try to reverse-information the phone number, but it came up blank. I couldn't find an address on any of the search sites. Not that it would have made a bit of difference.

I went into the shower and scrubbed myself clean. I shaved. I pulled on a pair of jeans and a *Slaughtered* T-shirt before I realized the horrible symbolism of it. When I saw myself in the full-length mirror on the back of my bedroom door, I flushed with guilt and exchanged it for a plain black American Apparel T-shirt without a logo.

Okay, that was good for half an hour. I still had three and a half hours to wait before I could call Jumbo Jax and find out if he was for real.

I went down to the Boulevard and pulled in to Bobby's for an old school breakfast, heavy on fat and carbs and nitrites. The omelet was enormous, the bacon dripping with grease, and the breakfast potatoes sprinkled with melted orange cheese. It came with a steaming bagel that leaked butter all over the bread plate, looking like a last meal on Death Row. My belly squealed as the first bites struck home, but quieted as I continued to feast. I read the paper on my iPad, trying to take my time, but not able to comprehend a word. I flipped through the Calendar section to the weekend box-office report, angry to see that the top grossing films were all sequels and remakes. I wanted to be able to gloat that the ticket-buying public had gotten fed up with all that shit, but they hadn't. America was lapping it up and asking for more.

I was in the wrong business; I just wouldn't listen.

I looked up at the wall clock as the second-hand ground around its face in slow motion. It was almost eight o'clock: two more hours before I could call my new best friend. The butter and grease and unborn chickens and box-office mojo suddenly broke out in a fistfight in my stomach, and I ran into the men's room, dropping my drawers just in time to expel them in a sick, flatulent, watery stream. That was good for another ten minutes.

Physically and psychically evacuated, my body felt wrung out, empty, spindly and useless. In a sudden lurch, I vomited all that had not yet been digested into the sink in big yellow and brown chunks. Someone started knocking on the locked restroom door, and I washed the sweat off my face, and the puke off my chin. I flushed a couple of times, and ran the sink as much as I could, but the stench was foul and omnipresent. I ran my wet fingers through my hair, unlocked the door, and rushed past the business-suited, grey-haired geezer at the door, but not before I heard him exclaim, "Jesus!" and rush back into the restaurant. A rank cloud followed me back to my table, where I paid the bill with cash and left a healthy tip to make up for the stink I left in my wake.

Quivering, I climbed into the Beemer and made my way back up the hill to the house, running through the sprinklers, which had come on in my absence. I went back into my office and pored through the Facebook messages that had accrued since I'd left, but there was nothing new there worth my time. Tick. Tick. Tick. The digital clock on the iMac taunted me. I turned on the television and flipped through the channels of daytime broadcast TV, and it made me want to shoot myself. Every other channel had a courtroom show on, with white trailer trash and angry black folks screaming at one another in furious, self-righteous indignation, threatening and squawking with belligerent hands on massive hips: slender, shaven-headed dudes who stole cars and money from their triple-sized ex-girlfriends; an ex-con sleeping with the sister of his live-in girlfriend, knocking her up, and denying all responsibility;

an eighteen-year-old surfer boy claiming he'd awakened at a sleepover at his best friend's house, only to find the friend's naked, obese mother riding him like a pony; he was asking for five thousand dollars for emotional distress. My, how time doesn't fly when you're not having fun.

Somehow the eternity of two hours passed, and I picked up the hard-line phone and placed my call. The guy picked up on the second ring.

"Hi," I said. "This is James Turrentine. Chase Willoughby's husband."

"I figured," the voice on the other end of the line said.

"You said you saw my wife the night before she was killed?"

"That's right. And you said you've got a hundred-thousand-dollar reward?"

"I did."

"How do I go about getting this hundred-thousand-dollar reward?"

"By giving me any information that will lead to the capture of her murderer." There was a long silence on his end, and I heard traffic around him. The connection was too clear to be mobile; I was guessing that this was a pay phone. I looked again to see if the fourth digit was a nine, and it was. That's a pretty good clue.

"So it's not something you'd pay for in cash today."

"I'm not an idiot. Do you have information for me?"

Another silence, and then: "What will you pay today?"

"It depends on what you have to tell me."

"I don't want to talk over the phone."

"I'll come to you if you want," I offered.

"Well I'm sure as shit not coming to you." He huffed a mirthless laugh, and I could hear his mind ticking. "How quick can you get to Palm Springs?" he asked me.

Palm Springs. The desert. The cocksucking, motherfucking desert.

"Two, two and a half hours."

"Meet me at the Starbucks at Palm Canyon Drive and Tahquitz Way at noon."

"Will you be the guy in the white carnation?"

"I'll recognize you."

Then he hung up. I ran out the door and into the BMW, squealing out of the driveway, away from Woodland Hills and back to the goddamned desert.

Ω Ω Ω

I hated the monotony of the road, the listless, sunburned, featureless sprawl of the grey California desert in particular. The sky wasn't even blue, just a bleached, sweltering white. No color, no flavor, no life. I couldn't bear to even listen to the radio, so it was a quiet, almost insufferably dull drive: two hours of heat and blacktop and a stomach that wouldn't settle. Jesus, how I hated the desert, and hoped never to have to go there again. The desert is where you go to die.

I passed the faded concrete dinosaurs, which had been almost completely obscured by fast food restaurants, and knew I was close; once I was on Route 111, all that was left was a sour stomach and anticipation. In all probability, this guy was just an opportunistic asshole. But there was a chance that he could provide information, that I could cut the line between Chase's death and the law enforcement agencies who had no personal commitment to her story. Perhaps Jumbo Jax could help me justify my place on the planet, unlikely as it seemed.

It was about five minutes past noon when I found a parking place right on the street, cater-corner from the Starbucks at Palm Canyon Drive and Tahquitz Way. Finding an energy I thought had left me forever, I bounded from the car and ran through traffic to the opposite corner, where a dozen or so patrons sat comfortably in chairs in front of the coffeehouse. An old woman hiding behind a new facelift and enormous Donna Karan sunglasses sipped her vanilla macchiato as her enormously overweight black Chihuahua snored at her feet. A May-December gay couple tried to keep their voices down as they fought about their financial arrangement, the younger one telling him to take his goddamn car back as he held ice to a swollen eye and bleeding nose. A massively obese black man with one leg sat in a wheelchair with a "Pleeze Help God Blees You" sign planted in a coffee can in his lap. A couple of bearded, liver-spotted old men played chess in total silence, and a table full of MILFs and their attendant spoiled, squalling, begging offspring drew dirty looks. None of them seemed like they might bear the moniker of Jumbo Jax.

I stepped inside and prickled into gooseflesh in the blast of conditioned air. I stepped right up to the counter and ordered a giant iced tea. As I waited for my drink, movement from the corner caught my eye. A guy in sunglasses, a long-sleeved black shirt, black jeans, and worn, buckled, calf-high black boots, maybe twenty-two, twenty-three years old, flicked his hand to draw my attention. If I'd been casting Jumbo Jax for an episode of *Slaughtered*, I'd have passed on this guy for being too on-the-nose. I grabbed my tea and joined him at the tiny corner table. As I started to sit, he spoke, arresting my movement into the chair:

"I'll have a Venti Java Chip Frappuccino. And a blueberry muffin." I nodded, went back to the counter and ordered, then returned and took a seat opposite him.

"Jumbo Jax?" I asked, not really needing an answer, but wondering what the fuck I should call him.

"Jaxon." Nobody extended a hand for shaking, which was fine by me. I didn't really want to touch this guy.

"James," I said.

"I know."

His glasses were tinted so dark that I couldn't see his eyes. I wished he couldn't see mine.

"So," I began, waiting for him to pick up the conversation. When he proved unwilling, I continued. "You saw my wife on the night she died?"

The barista called out "James!" and rather than answer, Jaxon nodded to her. I went to the counter, collected his breakfast, and returned to the table, laying it out for him.

He took a long suck, draining a good third of his drink.

"You saw my wife on the night she died," I repeated.

"Several times," he answered, trying to be all tough and mysterious. He was no tougher than the whipped cream that topped his Frappuccino.

"Here in Palm Springs?"

"Did you bring your wallet?"

"Do you want to do this here?" I asked him.

"Why not?"

I could think of reasons, but if this cocky little asshole couldn't, that was fine with me. He took a big bite of muffin, and crumbs stuck to his three days of beard as he chewed. I pointed to the corners of my mouth, and he wiped his with the back of his arm, smearing blueberry residue up the length of his sleeve.

I blocked the view from the other customers with my back, reached into my pocket, and laid out a pile of cash on the table in front of him.

"How much is that?" he asked.

"A thousand bucks," I answered.

"Where's the other ninety-nine thousand?"

God, this desert hipster was an idiot. It was obvious that he thought he was pretty hot shit, but if he were in LA, he'd never get a callback.

"The reward thing works like this," I told him. "You give me information that leads to the arrest and conviction of Chase's killer, and then you collect, upon his conviction."

"That could be years!"

"It could."

"Fuck that." He stood up and reached for the money. I grabbed his hand.

"Uh uh," I said. "That's a down payment. But you haven't told me shit." I took the money and started to stuff it back in my pocket.

"Wait a minute!"

I sat back down, and he did the same.

He looked at me, looked at my bulging pocket.

"A thousand bucks?" he asked. "That's it?"

"To start with," I replied. "But I'll pay more if the information is worth it."

"It's worth it."

"Prove it." I put the money back on the table, my hand laid atop the pile of bills. "Did you see Chase here in Palm Springs that night?" It certainly jibed with what Danny, the waiter at Kate Mantilini, had told me: girls' night out in the desert.

"Yes."

I lifted my hand, and he grabbed the money, jamming it into his own pocket.

"Where?" I asked.

"Couple a' places," he answered.

"Like, for instance?"

"Like, for how much?"

"You don't know much about civic duty, do you?"

"No. I'm not so good with abstract concepts."

Wiseass. I took a moment to think, to consider. I had taken a plunge, had chosen to believe that he was telling the truth. It was time to throw in all the marbles.

"Is there a Citibank in town?"

"Yeah. Down the street on East Palm Canyon."

"Great. Come with me, and I'll give you another four thousand dollars to tell me everything you know about Chase's final night. That's five thousand total," I added, just in case he wasn't good at math.

"That's not as much as I was hoping."

"It's five percent of a hundred thousand. And it's up front. No waiting." The machinery in his brain worked slowly. "Or I could just go to the cops. I know they'd be happy to talk to you, and they wouldn't pay you a fucking cent."

"You got a car?" he asked.

"No, we'll take my wings." He looked confused. "I'm in the Beemer right across the street."

"Cool. By the way, I really dig *Slaughtered*. It's really sick."

Great. My audience. My fan base. I'll have a grande double-shot Rat Poison, please.

We ditched Starbucks, went to the bank, and I took out the cash, which he was all grabby for. "Information first, right?"

He stared at the money, lusting for it. It gave me a sense of power; I was usually the one with my hand out.

"I'm hungry," he non-sequitured. "How about you?"

I didn't think I'd ever be hungry again, but I was eager to get out of the baking Palm Springs sun. "Where do you want to eat?"

"You been to Rick's?"

Ω Ω Ω

Rick's was just a diner, nothing more, nothing less, a place that only served breakfast and lunch. All of the gay male clientele was seated in front; the hetero crowd and any party with a female had all been shunted to the rear of the place. I didn't know what to think when the host put us right in the front window.

I just had an Arnold Palmer, but Jaxon ordered a steak.

"Where did you see my wife?" I asked him again. He thrummed his fingers on the table. I didn't want to fuck with this shit any more, so I pulled out the cash and laid it on the table in front of him. A greedy grin washed over his face as he took the money and tucked it away.

"A couple of places."

"And those places were…" I led him.

"A club called Alternate Route, first. I recognized her there. I told her I used to watch *The Crazy Frazees* when I was a kid, and that seemed to piss her off."

I doubted that Chase was pissed off because he liked her show when he was a boy. Surely there was something this dunderhead wasn't saying.

"Was she alone?"

"No," he answered. "She was with this hot little redhead."

Antoinette McLoughlin. It was all tying together, I just didn't know how. But this guy, this Jaxon in Black, was telling the truth. I didn't waste my five thousand dollars, even though I couldn't afford it.

"She left pretty quick after that. Like she was on the rag or something."

I can't say I blamed her. This guy needed to work on his first impressions, and all the ones that followed.

"Did you follow her?"

"I wouldn't call it 'following' her, not really."

"But you watched where she went and then you went there, too."

"Exactly. She made me curious. I was a big fan when I was a kid. And, you know, your wife was really hot." He smiled at me, and I wanted to shove that steak knife in his throat.

I quelled my repulsion and kept my outward calm. "Where did she go next?" I queried.

"To the Riviera Hotel. She seemed to get pretty cozy with the singer in the band, the Sinatra guy."

"How do you mean, 'cozy'?"

"You know, slow-dancing-with-him cozy."

"Kissing cozy?"

"Yeah, kissing cozy. I think he took her to his room."

This didn't sound like Chase to me, and I could feel my face going warm and red. I hadn't really known Chase in a long time, I guess. I tried to just ask the questions, not feel the scorn, the disregard for our marriage, as pointless and hollow as it had become.

Fighting down my gorge, I asked him, "What happened next?"

"That was the last I saw of her there. I assumed she and the Sinatra dude hooked up, and I just booked. There was no reason to hang around any longer. I thought she kinda liked me, that maybe I had a shot, but once the singer got her, well, that's like game over, isn't it? Chicks love singers."

I could feel my throat constrict. I did my best to keep my voice level, unengaged.

"And that was the last you saw of her?"

"That was the last I saw of her at the Riviera." He obviously had more to say, so I waited for it. I wasn't going to do him the pleasure of asking him to continue. He couldn't keep his mouth shut, anyway.

"I went back up to Palm Canyon to see if anything was happening. I sure didn't expect to see her there, and so quick. I guess the thing with the singer didn't work out, after all." He was smiling as he related this to me, the dead woman's cuck-olded husband.

"Where did you see her?"

"On the street. Walking. Maybe she was looking for her friend, because she was by herself."

"Where did she go?"

"It didn't seem like she was going any place in particular, she was just walking around town." A shadow flashed across his face at this point, like he was glossing over something in-criminating.

"Just walking around town," I repeated.

"Pretty much."

"And that was it?"

"Not exactly," he said. "There's a punchline."

"Okay," I told him. "Make me laugh."

"She ended up in a carpet-munchers bar." The smug look on the little bastard's face made me want to cut it off and feed it to a cat. "The Clamshell."

"And that's the last place you saw her?"

"Yes. And as I'm not especially welcome in a dyke-bar kind of establishment, I made a hasty exit. I went back to the Riviera and got lucky with this German tourist chick with a shaved head and lots of tattoos and piercings. Kind of hot, but the metal made a lot of noise."

He took the money back out of his pocket and counted it as I watched him, seething.

"The last place you saw Chase was at a lesbian bar called the Clamshell."

"That's right."

"Take me there," I said. He was a bit taken aback.

"I doubt they're going to be open in the middle of the day."

"I don't care. Take me there. You got something else to do?"

He sopped up the last drippings of the steak with a wad of bread, gulped it down with a couple glugs of his Coke, and belched proudly before following me out to the car.

Ω Ω Ω

Jaxon directed me to the Clamshell, which was only a few blocks away. The street seemed sandblasted in the harsh midday sunlight, surrounded by empty storefronts and sandy, vacant lots. Jaxon seemed a little nervous when I pulled up in front of the place, caffeine jitters animating him like a stop-motion puppet. It was a big change from the mellow, couldn't-give-a-shit hipster I'd been talking to for the last hour or so. I set the parking brake and he ran his fingers through his purposeful dishevelment.

"Well, if you don't need me anymore..."

I didn't. Frankly, I was glad to be rid of the little prick. He smelled like cigarettes, and the leather upholstery was absorbing his reek. I guess he expected me to stop him, because he paused and looked at me when he opened the passenger door, but as far as I was concerned, he was already gone. He slammed the door and left me alone. In my natural state.

I looked at the Clamshell, wondering what pearly secrets it held for me. Unsteady in nervous anticipation, I got out of the car, locked it up, crossed the sidewalk, and grabbed the handle of the Clamshell's door. I pushed, but it didn't give. But when I pulled, it opened wide.

The place was dark and empty, tomb-like. The wedge of sunlight that stretched from the doorway in front of me was like an invasion, curdling the cool, wicked darkness with disinfecting brightness. I entered and let the door fall shut behind me, and my eyes had to adjust to the resumption of dim.

"Hello," I called out, wincing as the word left my mouth. Too loud: this room was meant for whispers. There was no reply, and I stepped deeper within the Clamshell, which was lit only with neon signs advertising beer, mostly for brands I'd never heard of. Since I'd quit drinking four years ago, I don't pay much attention to the brews of the moment, micro or macro. I walked to the bar, and noticed a cigarette burning in a Molson's ashtray, smoke coiling like a charmed cobra all the way to the ceiling. Just smoke, no smoker. I took a seat at the bar and tapped on the old, dented mahogany with my knuckle. "Hello?" Still nothing. It was as if all life had been zapped away by overflying alien life forms.

Suddenly, a door opened on the opposite side of the room behind me, and with the click of the light switch, the tavern was flooded with harsh, nasty fluorescent light. It was immediately apparent that I didn't want to see a nighttime place in the middle of the day: the corners were crusted with grime and beer residue and God-knows-what-else. I whirled on my barstool and locked eyes with the most masculine woman I've seen this side of the Olympics, wheeling a dolly loaded down with cases of beer. She looked leathery, not old but crumpled by constant desert sun. She dropped her load with a grunt and was about to pick up the three cases from the top of the stack when she locked eyes with me. The cases fell with a crash, throwing shards of brown glass and plumes of imported beer across the floor in foamy waves.

"Sorry," I apologized.

"What the fuck are you doing here?"

I didn't yet have an answer to that; I was still stunned by the blast of light and the bulging, sinewy, over-testosteroned arms on this creature. But in a moment, I saw a response to me in her eyes with which I was becoming increasingly familiar: recognition. Nothing like the celebrity of being married to somebody who was a little bit famous and had been messily killed. Oh, to be obliviously unknown again.

"First of all," she told me, narrowing her eyes in an attempt to intimidate me, which she did, "we don't open until four. And second, this is a club for women. In case you didn't know. And I'm guessing you've got a dick."

I tried to squint back in my best Clint Eastwood impression, but it felt silly. It made her smile.

"I'm just looking for information," I said.

"We're all outta that. But we've got it on backorder."

I don't know if she wanted me to laugh, but I didn't. And neither did she.

"I'm Chase Willoughby's husband," I said. It's all I ever was and all I ever will be, I suppose.

"I know. I recognize you from the TV."

Her grey eyes never blinked, content just to penetrate me, pin me to the bar like a butterfly against velvet.

"I was told that she was seen here the night that she was…"—it was still hard for me to say it—"killed."

That word hung like a poison cloud in the silence that followed. Giving it time to evaporate, she looked down at the lake of beer that covered the floor, then back up to me, letting me know that this was all my fault.

"Your wife? In a dyke bar?" She looked unconvincingly credulous. "That sounds strange."

"To me, too." I could play dense, as well. "Were you working here that night? Did you see her?"

"Chase Willoughby? The TV star? Here at the Clamshell?" I could see that this lady hadn't shaved in a couple of days. And that tattoo on her arm looked like she got it in San Diego when the fleet came in.

"Yes. Was she here? Did you see her?"

"We don't get many TV stars at the Clamshell."

"I don't doubt it," I said. "But just that one is all I'm interested in."

"Who told you they saw her here?"

"A little birdie," I snarked.

"Your little birdie is full of shit."

That might have been true, but I could tell she was lying.

THIRTEEN

What the fuck happened to my head?

I felt weighed down, logy, as if I were wearing a lead fat suit. My head throbbed with a searing, sharp pain like I'd never felt before. My mouth felt thick and dry, as if stuffed with gauze, which it turned out it was. My eyelids were so heavy that I couldn't lift them; I felt like I was waking up from a hundred-year sleep. My neck could not support the weight of my newly hydrocephalic skull, and it rocked from side to side. My body was vibrating, jostled, in motion. I could tell I was in a vehicle, but I just couldn't pry my eyes open to prove it.

My stomach was hollow, empty and protesting, but I still wanted to vomit. The gauze scraped against the back of my tongue, igniting my retch reflex, but nothing came up but the groans. I gagged, and the gauze—or whatever the hell it was—was ejected from my mouth and onto my lap with a sick, wet plop.

I kept struggling to open my eyes, but they just kept rolling back in my head, each heartbeat inflating them with merciless agony. We hit a bump, and I thought I was made of glass, because I shattered. Dull numbness had given way to acute sensitivity, and every cell of my being exploded with hurt. I lifted my head from its leeward tilt and finally got my lids to lift. I was surrounded by darkness. Wherever we were, it was not on the planet Civilization. Aside from the tall light poles that whipped past every so often, the expanse beyond the passing asphalt was dark, arid, nonexistent. I tried to squeeze my hands into fists, and they filled with the sparkles of disappearing anesthetic.

"Morning, Sunshine," said a voice from my left, and I turned to look, but it took a while to focus. This was my brain on drugs. Certainly not morning. Black as pitch. Dark as my dreams.

My head lolled as I tried to make my brain function, to remember that eyes see, ears hear, and mouths speak. It dawned on me that I spoke English, but I was afraid to try it out. My eyes rolled again, independent of one another, and then settled into place and found unified peace that allowed them to focus.

The thing at the wheel was watching me, with an occasional glance at the road. I had seen this person before, I just couldn't remember where.

"How ya feeling? Head hurt?"

The army of my brain was starting to build a functioning battalion. I knew this face. This was a woman, and her name was Frank. "Frank?" I said, but it came out "Fwuh?"

There was a sort of smile on her face, but it lacked joy or humor.

"It'll go away soon, Pretty Lady." She looked at me, from my eyes to my feet, and all stops in between. A car rushed by from the opposite direction, and she threw a glance and righted her navigation, but then her eyes returned to me. The veil of unconsciousness was slowly lifting.

"You okay?"

I shook my head, but it hurt. I definitely was not okay. I looked down to see that my hands and ankles were bound with sleeves torn from the same red plaid shirt.

"You are a pretty one, aren't you?" She said it like an accusation. "Is that what you're all about? You're all about pretty, aren't you?"

I was not equipped to answer that.

She reached over and rubbed a thick, dry thumb across my mouth, scraping my lips like sandpaper, and pulling it away with a smear of lipstick. She put it in her mouth to taste it, then spat on the floor of the vehicle. She turned to glare at me with undisguised hatred, and I wondered what I did to earn her obvious ire.

"You look like a little doll," she said as she stared me down. It was not said with affection. "You don't even look human." She turned back to the road, and I watched as stretches of midnight desert flew past the windshield. I could see that we were in a pickup truck, shining and well maintained despite its obvious age, reflecting the freeway lights as we raced beneath them. Her face seethed with anger, and she gripped the steering wheel in fists that were white with fury. In a sudden burst of rage, her hand shot out, slamming her fist painfully down on my thigh, then pulling it away just as quickly.

"Ow!" I screamed.

She threw a glance my way, then back to the road. It seemed like a Dr. Strangelove kind of thing, a sudden lack of control. She put her left hand over her right and clenched the wheel tight, muttering something to herself that I couldn't understand.

I looked away from her, out onto the deserted highway as it hurtled past us, still reeling, still groggy. I saw two glittering spots in the darkness ahead, which grew rapidly into a shape, furry, four-legged, trapped in the headlights. A coyote stared at us as it straddled the double yellow line, a frightened statue, until Frank narrowed her eyes and gunned the engine and plowed over it at eighty-five miles an hour. The impact threw me against the window and my head exploded in a white blast of light that quickly faded to black.

Ω Ω Ω

I roused for a moment as the truck slowed and the gears downshifted noisily. I felt a thorny hand push my head down against the seat, keeping a tight hold on my mouth. I opened my eyes and could only see up, just in time to see the California-Arizona border roll past. We entered the Grand Canyon State without stopping, and a whirlpool of unconsciousness sucked me back under.

Ω Ω Ω

I woke again as the truck pulled off onto gravel, slowing to a crawl as Frank turned the wheel with a weird little knob that let her control it one-handed. I lifted a hand to the sore spot on my forehead, forgetting it was tied to its mate. Both hands rose to press against the goose egg above my brow, and when I pulled it away, it was painted with my blood. I didn't need to see that; I was woozy enough already. The pickup slowly ground across the rough, pebbled parking lot, and her face was illuminated by the sickly green neon lights that spelled MOTEL. I couldn't make out the name of the motel; it was too long and confusing, and the blue neon wouldn't come into focus anyway.

She eased the truck around the back of the low row of seedy-looking cabins, hiding it in their illicit shadows. There were no other vehicles parked there; I don't even know if the place was open for business. As she ground to a halt, I reached for the door with my bound hands, but there was no handle on the inside. She noticed my move and silently shook her head. As my consciousness returned, I wished myself unsuccessfully back to oblivion.

"Where are we?" I asked, astounded that the words actually came out the way they were intended.

Frank looked at me, and let out a long breath through her nostrils. Without saying a word, she yanked the parking brake, opened her door, then reached in and scooped me up in her muscular, manly arms. I tried to struggle, but I had no strength, so she carried me effortlessly across the gravel, blue moonlight shadow puppets of us following close behind, to the front of the empty, quiet cabins, and kneed open the door to room number four.

Once inside, she closed the door behind her, then dropped me onto the forlorn double bed, raising a cloud of dust and a screech of bedsprings. She stared at me as I lay there, terrified.

"What are we doing here?"

Her face crinkled into a bitter smile. "I'm admiring you," she said. She stood at the end of the bed looking down on me, not tall but powerfully built, her hands on her hips, breathing raggedly through her mouth. She shook her head again. When she reached down for me, I tried to kick her away with my feet, but she just batted at them, and my body tumbled backwards over my head. She slapped me, and I started to cry. She grabbed the bodice of my dress and yanked it violently open, revealing the silk bra underneath. She slid her finger under the strap and snapped it painfully against my tender skin.

"How much did that cost?"

I don't know why it made her angry, so I lied. "I don't know. It was a gift."

"I'll bet it was." She snorted, scowled and shook her head. She ran her hand through my hair, then gave it a good yank before she pulled it away. "Are you a woman?" I was confused; I had no idea what she meant. She reached for my face, then pulled her hand away before she made contact. Then she kicked the bed.

"*I said, are you a woman?*" She raised a fist over my face as I cowered.

"Yes!" I answered. "Yes! Of course I'm a woman!"

She reached for me again, then pulled her hand away, fighting some kind of urge to touch me with an equal desire to hold herself back.

"Are you a woman or are you a toy? Are you a woman or are you a fantasy? Are you a woman or are you a love doll?" When I didn't respond, she lifted the bottom of the bed and dropped it heavily to the floor.

"I'm a woman!"

She went to the door and pounded against it with both fists, then stormed back to hover over me on the bed.

"No you're not," she whispered, drawing right up to my face and spreading her hot, wet words all over me. "You're not even real!" I tried to pull my head back away from hers, but she grabbed it and held it tightly in place, looking at my eyes, my hair, my mouth. Suddenly, she pressed her hard, dry, cracked lips against mine, darted her tongue against them, then pulled away in seeming disgust.

"You're just Hollywood, aren't you? Pure temptation!"

I started to cry, horrified at this furious creature that hated me for no reason I could understand.

"What are you doing to me?" I managed to sob.

She leaned down over me, brought her face close to mine, and breathed deeply through her flaring nostrils.

"You smell like a fucking whorehouse," she said with contempt.

I cowered, but she wouldn't let me, holding me by the neck against the bed. I choked, and she eased back a little, but kept me pinned to the bed.

I was terrified. "My friend will be looking for me..." I said.

"Who, the little redheaded pixie? I've already seen her. She gave me her card. Told me to call if I spotted you."

Her grey eyes were wild; despite the darkness, her pupils remained tiny, mad pinpoints of black surrounded by mono-chromatic, clenched irises. She looked like she was fighting de-mons, but the demons were winning.

"Do you know how disgusting you are? You're just candy! You let them make you into their toy, their plaything, their little dollycake. Do you know how that hurts us?"

She tore open my dress, pulled on it until I rolled out of it and onto the floor, wearing only my bra, cowering behind my hands. She picked me up with a rough yank and threw me back down onto the bed on my stomach. She yanked the bra apart, then rolled me onto my back, straddling me in her rough Lee jeans and pinning my arms to the bed. When I tried to fight her off, she backhanded me across the face. I started to get hys-terical, but it only made her madder.

She stared down at my naked body, her face doing battle with lust and disgust. She reached down with both her hands and squeezed my breasts, hard, and I squealed in pain.

Immediately, she jumped off of me, turning away from me, seemingly revolted with herself.

"I didn't want to do that!" she said, going to the window, seething, her fists pulsing.

"Then why did you?" I cried.

"Because you fucking made me!" She turned back to me, stormed over to the bed and kicked me hard in the side. "How much did those tits cost you?" she demanded. I couldn't answer, paralyzed by her volatile insanity. She reached down and grabbed one in both hands, squeezing hard.

"*How much did they cost you?*" she demanded again.

I was bound by hysteria, confusion, still fighting off the drugs. I just didn't understand what was going on, why I was so awful to her, why she hated me so much.

"They're mine!" I shouted.

"Bullshit!" she shouted back.

I just shook my head and she bent down and took the breast she was holding in her mouth and bit it hard. She jumped off of me again, went to the wall and pounded it with her fists, slammed her forehead against it over and over, fighting this horrible compulsion, and losing. There was only one way this could end.

She turned back to me, holding herself with her back against the wall. "Do you know how much I hate you?" she said, almost in a whisper. I didn't dare reply. "You were made for TV, you're not even real. You're just artificial sex and temptation, a cartoon, the invention of horny men to satisfy their selfish carnal cravings, an affront to women. Makeup and plastic surgery and hair dye and sexy underwear, just to make us want you but we can't have you. You make us all ugly. You make us all unsatisfied, because we can't have the beautiful doll, the empty fucking Barbie doll that only exists on TV. Well, *I* don't want you! You hear me? I don't even want you, I fucking hate you, you ugly bitch!"

She came closer to me, standing over me again, blocking the moonlight that was trying to creep in past the tattered curtains.

"Do you even know what a real woman looks like?" she asked. She reached down and pulled her shirt over her head, towering over me in silhouette, then coming closer for me to look. She was muscled but wrinkled, the definition of her shoulders and biceps and chest creased. Her breasts barely existed over the muscles of her chest, long nipples pointing downward. A line of dark pubic hair climbed up from her jeans to her navel.

"You don't even have any hair on your cunt!" she spat. I turned my legs away, trying to hide my crotch from her, but she yanked them back, slapped her hand around me and shoving dry fingers into me, tearing the fragile flesh. I pulled back in the searing agony.

"Why?" she said. "Why do you want to look like a little girl? Why did you let them do that to you?"

She seemed to lose control, yanked my face to hers and stuck her revoltingly long tongue into my mouth, making me gag. She pulled away and slapped me, like it was all my fault. Then she pulled up my hands and pressed them against her chest, squeezing, making me feel them.

"That's what a woman is supposed to feel like!" she screamed into my ear.

Then she reached down again and grabbed me. "Not like plastic! Not like fucking balloons!"

"They're real!" I cried. "They're me!"

She let me go and took a step back. That's when I saw that there was some sort of worn leather sheath strapped to her belt. She reached down and unbuckled it with a loud snap. She took out a knife so sharp, so highly polished, that it gleamed, reflected her madness like a mirror.

"Let's just see," she said, and made a fist around its hilt and drew it across her chest. Then, flecks of white foam collecting in the corners of her mouth, she was upon me, the blade flashing across me and splitting me open.

FOURTEEN

I stood across the bar from this steely-eyed, ropy-muscled creature with the slicked-back peppery hair as she glared at me, unblinking, Venus on the Clamshell. The gloom was deadening; it was like I was facing off with a grizzly at the back of its cave. Silence hung between us like a curtain, and I watched the muscles of her jaw working.

"I don't believe you," I told her. "I think Chase was here."

I wasn't sure why that made her smile.

"I don't give a fuck what you think, Dick."

"Why are you lying to me?" I really wanted to know. It just didn't make any sense.

All of a sudden, her arm flashed up from below the bar, holding a sawed-off aluminum baseball bat with a leather strap through the hole at the end. She swung it so hard at my head that it whistled, and I instinctively threw up my arms in protection. It smacked against my right forearm with a percussive *crack*. She climbed over the bar, her expression fierce as an aboriginal warrior's. I swung my fist at her as hard as I could, landing a blow across her face that, despite feeling alarmingly creampuff, snapped her head to the side and shocked her. I wasn't very good at face-to-face confrontation, even verbally, but when it came to hand-to-hand combat, I was a writer not a fighter, hopelessly inexperienced and outmatched. Raising the bat high over her head, she charged me. I kicked up as hard as

I could, catching her in the crotch, sorry she didn't have family jewels to shatter. It had little effect other than to put off her attack for a few more seconds. She slammed the weapon against my ribcage and kicked me in the stomach, knocking the wind out of me and throwing me into the middle of the room where there was nothing to grab. I felt the beer on the floor seeping through my shoes as I stood, trying not to quake in them.

She glared at me with fierce black-and-white hatred, breathing hard through her nose like a cartoon bull. She was silent, overflowing with hatred as she stood there, hunched, her hands flexing before her. Then she charged me, and I crossed my hands in front of my face. She swung again, but so did I, kicking laterally at her legs, knocking them out from under her and making her slip on the wet floor and crash onto her face and belly. She screamed, and when she pulled herself up, I knew why: a huge shard of brown bottle-glass was embedded in her cheek, lacerating open an additional mouth, which bled profusely. There were other slices in her shirt, new wounds oozing freely. She yanked the glass out of her face, saw it covered with her blood, and threw it at me, missing. But that was the end of my luck; with an animalistic snarl, she stomped toward me, her slips on the beer-soaked floor not slowing her down, swinging the bat as hard as she could, slamming it against my head from the left, then from the right, then from the left again, each collision raising a universe of stars before I was overcome and slipped from consciousness.

Ω Ω Ω

All I knew was that I was on my back, and that there were sharp rocks underneath me. My olfactory senses were ignited before my eyes opened. The acrid, pungent stench of fire woke me up, and when I tried to pry my eyes open, only one of them worked, and that one only barely. My head throbbed, felt lumpy and pulpy. My eyelashes peeled apart, sticky from my own congealing blood. I looked up into the towering, heavily bearded palm trees, clustered around a stream in some kind of desert oasis, no doubt one of the Indian canyons on the cusp of the city of Palm Springs. The pink sun played hide-and-seek just over the colorless, rocky crest of the San Jacinto Mountains behind them, but orange flames roared up and obscured my view.

A work boot kicked me in the head, and I turned to catch the rough, determined smile of the madwoman from the Clamshell glaring at me from overhead in my cyclopean view.

"What the fuck, lady?" I managed to get out.

She just kicked me in the ribs, which probably cracked, I don't know. I already hurt everywhere, and it was all unbearable. When I tried to pull away, I discovered I was bound by a rough hemp rope, which held me immobile. I squirmed like a caterpillar, kicking and struggling, but she just kicked me again, pushing me toward the raging bonfire she had built.

The desert surrounding us was vast and desolate, formations of dull tan rock defying gravity, pockets of oasis palms tucked into the mountain crevasses here and there. The creek was at its summertime trickle, and I wondered why I gave a shit.

She kicked me again, and I rolled, one full circle closer to the fire, feeling the heat sear my tender, swollen, bleeding face. I was destined to burn to ash, to a dust scattered by blazing Santa Ana winds, erased from the planet without a trace. I forced myself to roll back, away from the inferno, but she just planted her heel in my side, and shoved me back. Then did it again, and I was just feet from the flames.

"Why are you doing this?"

That just pissed her off, and she kicked me in the head again.

"Why did you kill Chase?"

All that got me was another kick, rolling me yet closer to the fire, which felt like it was cooking me from just a foot or two away. I was covered in sweat, could feel myself baking.

The rage that flooded her face told me she was through teasing. She planted her heel against my shoulder, and shoved with all her considerable might. I screamed as I rolled into the fire, impossibly hot burning desert branches sizzling as my flesh rolled over them. Using all the strength I could summon, I kept rolling, across the fire and out the other side. I could smell burning hair, see the flames charring my clothes, and kept rolling across the sand until I had put it all out. I hacked on the grit in my mouth, barely able to breathe. Oily smoke welled from the fire, and I could smell me-meat scorching. The burns were agonizing.

Infuriated, she ran through the fire and stomped on me. She put her arms under my body and shoved, rolling me back into the burning branches. Once again, I was able to keep rolling to the other side, acquiring new fires to put out in the sand, new wounds that blistered and popped instantly, the hair on my head ablaze. I rolled, I extinguished the flames, and I laughed, not because it was funny but because it was so ridiculous, and it pissed her off so much. With a simian roar, she strode back through the flames like one of Satan's minions, reached down, and picked me up in her arms. She lifted my objecting, wriggling body high, allowing me the opportunity to ram my battered face into the nape of her neck, where I bit as hard as I could, tearing at her, ripping out a huge chunk of her creased, suntanned flesh, and unleashing a spurting fountain of her own blood to spatter my face.

She screamed, dropped me in a heap, and slapped both hands to her gouting neck. I kicked her legs and she dropped face first onto the fire. I rolled on top of her as she screamed into the scarlet branches, using my weight to pin her there as flames shot up around us. Her blood was still shooting from the hole in her neck, hissing as it hit the burning branches. I could feel the fire burning past her, the flames licking at me and tasting me, but not feeding on me like they fed on her. She choked on fire and smoke, her lungs quickly scorched, her screams drying up and dying out. Her skin bubbled and seared and I rolled off of her before it could consume me as well.

She went still as the voracious fire devoured her, and I watched from a few feet away. The nauseating stench of human barbecue filled the desert air, and as the blaze reached high into the sky, the sun began its final descent behind the mountains, turning the sky, the clouds, and the desert itself a dramatic shade of pink before it settled into a purple that signaled the end of another day.

The skin on my left arm was scorched and festering. The right had been fractured by this crazy woman's bat. Half of the hair had been burned off my scalp, and there was a spot on my ass where my pants had melted into it. It was excruciating to fight against my bonds, but the fire had eaten at the rope as well, and once my force met the weakness of a single burned spot, it finally fell away, and I was able to escape its grasp.

I was able to stand, able to watch the cremation of Chase's murderer as the flesh melted away from the bones, which were turning black as the flames chewed on them, eventually sure to leave them unrecognizable as dust. The fire wouldn't die out anytime soon, and I liked that. It seemed to flare brighter as the sky blackened and the stars awoke. A full moon was in place, but its blue glow was weak against the fire.

Ashes to ashes and all that shit.

I would never know why this woman, this monster, this bastardization of humanity had taken Chase's life. But whatever the reason, there's no way it could ever make sense to me.

I was burned and battered and a complete mess, but I was alive. I didn't deserve it, but I was alive and Chase was dead. I stood here under a cruel desert sky, the smell of death ever-present, a body burning at my feet, and I was alive. I had taken the life of Chase's murderer, but I felt no satisfaction. This creature may have taken Chase's life, but I couldn't help but feel that it was me who killed her. I had dreamed of avenging Chase's death, and perhaps I had, at least technically, but it didn't feel like a victory. All I knew was that I had loved Chase a long time ago, and loved her again anew, but it didn't do anybody any fucking good.

I felt no pity for the body that was being consumed by the fire, but I felt no heroism, either. I was alive, I kept telling myself, but I didn't feel like it. And I certainly hadn't earned it.

Ω Ω Ω

The bonfire began to wane after a while, and a hot, arid breeze began to rise. The few clouds had cleared the wakening moon, and I looked up to see a pickup truck reflecting it from behind the grove of palm trees. I didn't want anything to do with it. Let someone who mattered find it and solve their own mystery. Mine now had an ending.

I could see the lights of Palm Springs in the distance, glowing like heaven. A hawk circled the fire that roasted and disintegrated the remains of the beast that killed my wife. It squealed, waiting for the flames to die down and allow it a cooked meal. *You can have it*, I thought.

My body burning and aching and my mind numb and vacant, I began the long walk through the desert and back into the Springs to collect my car and go back to the house that I once shared with the wife who belonged there much more than I did.

FIFTEEN

So I sit, home alone in Woodland Hills. Sometimes a tour bus will circle the cul-de-sac, titillating the Midwestern tourists on board with cautionary tales about Hollywood and the curse of stardom, how even the rich and beautiful are not beyond the reach of madness and murder. The death of my wife fell out of the headlines to join the pile of corpses stacked high with the likes of Jean Harlow, Marilyn Monroe, Jayne Mansfield, Sharon Tate, and the equally unfortunate victims of celebrity. Pretty high-falutin' company for the girl with the boobs in *The Crazy Frazees*.

My hair is starting to grow back over much of my scalp, but my arm and my face are sculpted in scar tissue, a scarlet letter well-earned in a life poorly lived. The feminine prettiness of my surroundings are a constant reminder of the beautiful, heart-broken woman who still haunts these walls in her death. Some-times I sleep—try to sleep—in her bed, the bed that used to be *our* bed, but I know I don't belong there, perhaps I never did. I know that we had been happy there, a long time ago, but knew I did not deserve memories so warm. The fights, the coldness, the bitter words, the loneliness that infested this little cottage had fouled it. This house had a pretty face, but it choked on its memories.

I often sit in Chase's studio, surrounded by the paintings of rage and pain, and wonder what kind of art she would have made if I had been someone else, someone who loved her back as deeply as she deserved. Hers was a beauty in a cage, briefly allowed to escape and flower, only to be darkened and soured by me. They say it takes two, but I know that that just isn't true.

In my office, the iMac only glares at me, daring me to take up the gauntlet and fight the good fight. But I am cowed by it; I sit bathed in its accusatory glow, unable to type, unable to think, unable to create. I just feel tired, empty.

I miss Chase Willoughby, and only wish I had another chance to prove it.